# BREAKWATER

# BREAKWATER

CATHERINE JONES
PAYNE

FATHOM INK™

BREAKWATER



Published in the United States by Fathom Ink Press, Robinson, Texas.



Visit www.fathominkpress.com for more information.

ISBN (paperback) 978-1-946693-00-6
ISBN (ebook – EPUB) 978-1-946693-01-3
ISBN (ebook – MOBI) 978-1-946693-02-0

Cover Design: Kirk Douponce, Dog Eared Design.
Interior Design: Chris Bell, Atthis Arts LLC.
Author Photo: Steven Noreyko.

Visit the author at www.catherinejonespayne.com

Facebook: catherinejonespayneauthor
Twitter: @cjonespayne
Instagram: catherinejonespayne

For Mom, who insisted I keep my options open, pushed me to pursue the things I loved, and imparted in me a deep, abiding love for the ocean. I wouldn't be where I am today without your unflagging support for my crazy schemes.

And for Dad, whose voice I still hear in my head. You loved it when I wrote, and I know you'd be proud.

CHAPTER

# ONE

I clutched my dolphin's dorsal fin as she glided upward. Her muscles tensed, and a moment later we broke the surface and arched through the air. I giggled as I wrapped my left arm around Kiki's rubbery body.

Sunlight gleamed off my pearl-and-navy-coral engagement ring as we plunged back into the warm ocean waves. Tor had done well. Except for the ring on the finger of Prince Elias's new bride, I'd never seen its equal.

I grinned. *It doesn't really matter. It's just a ring.*

But I couldn't stop the little thrill of pride that warmed my body whenever I thought about it. It hardly seemed real that Tor, the youngest captain in the Royal Mer Guard, had sought me out.

I was never quite sure if the tingle in my stomach when I thought about my upcoming marriage flowed from excitement or nerves.

"He's a really good guy." I scratched Kiki's back. "Talented, intelligent, loyal to a fault. Everyone speaks well of him."

Kiki whistled at me. She could always sense when I felt nervous. I patted her side and sang to her in a soft, reassuring voice. "I'm alright, friend."

She didn't understand my words, of course, but my tone soothed her.

I clicked my tongue three times, and she turned around to swoop back toward the walls of Thessalonike. We soared over swaying coral and smooth sand, skirting past a royal-blue octopus and barely avoiding a snapping eel.

Within minutes, I spotted the spiraling coral that marked the entrance to the city. Sunlight filtered through the water, highlighting a school of blue-and-yellow fish.

Kiki quivered. I scratched her side and launched my body away from her, toward the city, and she charged the fish with a squeal of glee. The fish scattered, bolting for crevices in the reef.

With a smile, I decided I'd come out again to see her tomorrow. Now that I'd graduated, I had a few precious months of free time before I'd need to choose a career, and I intended to take full advantage of the opportunity.

Mother had promised to find me an apprenticeship with another advisor or a diplomat, but I doubted I could stomach politics for the rest of my life. I'd seen the way political games and half-truths wore on Mother.

But when I was out with Kiki, I didn't have to think about any of it.

I flicked my fin and barreled toward the gate, waving at the contingent of guards—five mermen and three mermaids—stationed at the entrance to the city. They nodded at me. I'd gone to school with three of them, and the others likely recognized me as Advisor Cleo's daughter.

In the middle, a couple of guards conversed with a two-legged, dark-haired figure clad in an ethereal robe. He stood a head shorter than either guard.

*What's a naiad doing out here?*

We had lived in uneasy coexistence with a small population of naiads for nearly ten years. They all worked in the city, mostly for wealthy mer. I didn't often see one at the gate. Then again, aside from the fishers and harvesters, few mer ever stirred outside the city.

I studied his small frame and short-cropped hair and realized that I recognized him. He worked in my friend Rhea's house.

Her mother must've sent him on an errand without regard for the hassle he'd get from the guards when he returned.

A whirlpool raged in my stomach. I started to swim past them but then changed my mind and approached the two guards.

"Excuse me?" I said. "Is there a problem?"

One of the guards glanced at me. "No problem, milady. Just making sure his story's straight."

"Why wouldn't it be?"

The guard's lips tightened. "We want to make sure he had a good reason for leaving the city. Can't be too careful these days."

"He works in a respectable house. I'll vouch for him," I said.

"Milady, with all due respect . . ."

I drew myself up to my full length, hoping the simple kelp wrap that stretched from my shoulders to my belly button wouldn't undermine my words. I hadn't planned on confronting the guards when I left the city dressed like a shopkeeper.

"Do you know who I am?" I enunciated each word like Mother would and hoped they wouldn't notice my gills flaring or sense my rapid heartbeat.

"Milady—"

"This naiad is in the employment of Lady Athanasia and Lord Zenon. Let him go on his way."

The guard's nostrils flared. "Yes, Lady Jade." He nodded brusquely at the naiad. "Go on."

As the naiad stepped away from the guards, he looked at me and mouthed, "Thank you."

I swam alongside him in silence until we reached the first canal inside the city. It was small and sparsely populated, but I figured he'd be fine on his own from here.

"Go in peace." I bowed.

He hesitated. "Milady, I—"

"Go in peace."

He smoothed his silvery-white gossamer robe. "And peace be upon you."

He bowed his head and placed his right fist on his heart, then turned and kicked off the coral seafloor with his legs. A fine white stream of bubbles rushed past me as he jetted away, and my hair billowed backward in the current he'd cast. Moments later, he disappeared around a corner.

Jealousy tugged at me as I watched him go. *Naiads don't have it easy in Thessalonike, but what I wouldn't give to be able to bend water like that.*

I nodded at the guards and drifted into the city. Taking time for water to filter over my gills, I let the sights and sounds of urban life wash over me again. When I turned the same corner the naiad had darted around, nervousness tugged at my chest.

I didn't like crowds.

Two fishmongers hawked their wares in the middle of the busy canal. Their haggling blocked a merchant, who struggled to maneuver around them with a food cart drawn by a dolphin a little smaller than Kiki.

It seemed like half the mer on the canal were children and teenagers younger than I was. School must have just gotten out. I'd spent longer on the reef than I'd planned to.

A handful of naiads dotted the crowd, conspicuous in their opalescent clothing—spun from the water itself, our seamstress Pippa said—and their short, bobbing movements.

If a canal was too crowded for a naiad to jet through on their own current, as the main canals usually were at this time of day, they had to walk. To me, at least, walking seemed like a terribly inefficient way to travel.

I turned down the canal toward my house. Memories of my father churned in my mind. *Not all the naiads are bad. Father would be proud that I confronted the guards.*

I flipped to the edge of the canal and swam upward,

alongside the single row of second-story shops where the crowd was thinner. Allowing a gentle current to carry me, I forced myself to relax, letting my anxiety fade.

Then I tensed again. *The party. I have to go to the party at Tor's parents' tonight.*

I groaned. After the encounter with the guards, I just wanted to curl up in a ball like a sea urchin.

*What will Mother say when she finds out I challenged the Royal Mer Guard? And for a naiad?*

I SLIPPED into my house through the back door and floated up the vertical blue corridor toward the sleeping chambers. My room, the second door on the left, sat next to my little brother's chamber and across the hall from my mother's.

I swept into my room and sank onto my sleeping hammock. Glancing at the tide glass, I sighed. *Only an hour before the party begins.*

"Jade?" Mother's voice floated up from the first level of the house.

"Yes?"

"Pippa finished your new wrap. You can wear it tonight if you'd like."

I glided toward the closet in the corner of my chamber and pulled out the new addition, a purple-and-blue chiffon piece. I could only imagine the fortune Mother had spent on the cloth.

*It really is lovely, though. I hope Tor likes it.*

After wrapping the chiffon in an intricate style around my torso and chest, I reached for my clamshell comb and teased the tangles from my fuchsia hair. I considered putting it up with clips but decided to leave it down.

Pursing my lips, I squinted at the reflection in my ornate oval mirror framed by whorls of gold and topped with a fleur-de-lis—my personal favorite shipwreck salvage. *Mother didn't pay overland trade prices for that, at least.*

The chiffon complemented my hair and looked vibrant against my deep brown skin, but something was missing. Perhaps a necklace would complete the outfit.

I dug through my jewelry box and landed on a simple pendant necklace—a shark tooth carved in the shape of a dolphin. Father had bought it for me shortly after I'd rescued Kiki.

Mother might disapprove—it wasn't fancy enough for the party, really, but I thought the overland jewels the other ladies wore looked silly. Privately, Mother thought so too, though she'd never admit it outside the house.

I glanced at my reflection in the mirror. *Good enough. After all, I'm already engaged. No need to flaunt my position anymore.*

I hesitated.

*But then again, I'll need one of these mer to apprentice me in the next few months.*

I added three strands of pearls—two black and one white—to the ensemble and then nodded at my reflection in approval.

With a grin, I looked at my ring. It didn't shine inside. The bioluminaries that coated the ceiling provided enough light to see comfortably but not enough to make anything gleam.

"Jade?"

I turned around to find a tall, elegant mermaid in my doorway.

"Rhea!" I squealed and rushed over to give her a hug.

"I *need* to see your ring!" She grabbed my left hand and gasped. "Oh, Jade. It's *exquisite*."

I fought back a smile. "I love it."

"And Tor's so dreamy."

"He'll be a good life partner, I think."

Rhea rolled her eyes. "So practical. He's *gorgeous*!"

I giggled. "Yeah. He really is."

"I need *every* detail about the proposal." She grabbed my arms and spun me around in a circle. "Did he really do it at Sapphire? I've only eaten there once. Father says it's too expensive." She rolled her eyes.

"He booked out the whole restaurant." A grin spread across my face. "We ate a five-course meal, and he read a poem he wrote for me."

Rhea covered her mouth and squealed.

"The server was supposed to bring out the ring with dessert, but she forgot."

"No!"

I winced at the memory. "Tor got really upset. He threatened to get her fired, but I set him straight."

Rhea looked in my mirror and smoothed her hair. "It's really sweet that he cared about everything being perfect." She grabbed a bracelet off my dresser, slid it on her wrist, and re-examined her reflection. "When's the wedding?"

I crossed my arms.

"What?" She set my bracelet back on the dresser and smoothed her black hair.

"Nothing. Wedding's in four months. His mother insisted it happen before storm season."

Rhea opened her mouth and then closed it again, her eyes wide. "How will you ever get it planned in time?"

"I don't know. It all seems fast to me. But I really do like him."

"What do you think of my wrap?" Rhea stretched out to show off the bright red cloth coiled around her torso.

"Lovely." I touched the fabric. "Feels like it'll last longer than mine, too."

"Yours is just *perfect*," she said. "We'll be the talk of the party."

I smirked, snatched a piece of stray seaweed off the windowsill, and flicked it at her with my fin.

"Oh!" She tugged a small pouch out of her wrap. "I nearly forgot. I need your advice on which necklace to wear." She pulled out a simple strand of pearls and a gaudy, emerald-studded gold choker. "I like the emeralds better, of course. They match my fin. But I'm worried it'll be too much."

"You already know what I'm going to say. I hate overland jewels, and you know it."

"I know." She sighed. "But do you think that *other* people will think it's too much? You have a great instinct for these things."

I eyed the necklace. "It is a *very* fancy party," I said at last.

"Oh, thank you!" She threw her arms around my neck. "I knew I could depend on your good sense! Now, come with me. I want to make sure we're there before Prince Theo. I absolutely *must* be talking with a handsome boy when he shows up so he sees that all the other boys want to talk to me."

"You were flirting with his older brother not two months ago."

She pouted. "Well it's not my fault Elias swam off and eloped with Keira. I can't help that there's only one prince left on the market. But Theo's a better pick, I think. Being queen sounds like such a bore."

"If we leave now, we'll be the first people there." I crossed my arms.

"All the better." She grabbed my arm and dragged me out of my room. "They're your in-laws now, so it's not rude, and we'll have the first go at the food."

AS WE crossed the threshold, I noted with chagrin that we were indeed the first people at the party. "Told you so," I whispered to Rhea.

"Jade, how delightful to see you," my new mother-in-law, Yvonna, said with a graceful smile.

I smiled back at her, trying to hide my discomfort. I never quite knew what to say to Yvonna. While she seemed pleased enough about the engagement, I'd always suspected she personally disliked me.

"I'm so happy to be here," I said. "You have such a lovely home."

It was true. Their home was twice as large as ours and decorated in the same style as the king's own reception hall. On the far wall, a trio of silver filigree dolphins—life-sized—chased a school of gold fish. Eight hundred and forty-five fish, to be precise. I'd counted them during a particularly insufferable party the month before.

We stared at each other in silence for a full ten seconds before I asked, "Is Tor around?"

"I believe he's in the courtyard. Go in peace."

"Thank you." I bowed. "Peace be upon you." I grabbed Rhea's hand, and we drifted toward the back door.

"Oh!" Rhea whispered in my ear, looking behind us just as her fingers curled around the door handle. "Philip's coming in! He's perfect for making Theo jealous. See you later."

She released the door handle and swooped down on poor, unsuspecting Philip.

I suppressed a smile.

*Leave it to Rhea.* With her beautiful face and all her machinations, it was a wonder she wasn't engaged yet. *Of course, she's not as well-connected as I am. I can't assume it's as easy for her as it was for me.*

With a final glance backward, I pushed my way into the well-appointed courtyard. Daring red anemone lined the walls just above three thin lines of bioluminaries that cast a romantic purple light on the scene.

I smiled and bit my lip. A battalion of tiny sea horses hovered around a feeder to my right.

Movement in the corner of my eye caught my attention, near Yvonna's prized fire coral garden at the corner of the house on the far side of the courtyard. I swam toward it. "Tor?"

When I reached the fire coral, I stopped short and locked eyes with Tor. My whole body trembled. In one arm, he held the dead body of a red-haired naiad girl.

# CHAPTER TWO

"What the depths?" My hand flew to my mouth.

Tor glanced at the naiad's body and back at me. "It isn't what you think. There wasn't anything going on between—"

"Wait, what?" I blinked.

He stopped talking.

"Did you . . ." I trailed off, almost unable to speak the thought out loud. "Did you *kill* her?"

He dropped her body to the seafloor and swam toward me. "I can explain."

When he cupped my chin in his hand, a shudder ran down my spine. I looked into his eyes and almost believed him.

"She was threatening the family. Telling all kinds of lies about my father's business—about my father—if I didn't give her money."

*But he didn't deny that he killed her.*

The horror of it all gripped my mind, and I had to focus to keep from shaking.

"Did. You. Kill. Her?"

"It was an accident. I was just trying to scare her. Please don't tell anyone." But his voice sounded flat.

"What have you *done?*" I dragged my fingers through my hair and suppressed the urge to vomit. My head spun.

"Why does it matter? She's just a naiad. You of all people shouldn't care."

Panic gripped my throat. "Just . . . a naiad?"

"Please, love."

I jerked away from his touch. "What? You'll kill me too if I say what you've done?"

"Of course not," he said, but his eyes narrowed in a way that sent cold fear hurtling through my chest. He raised his hand as if to caress my cheek, but the movement seemed jerky and forced.

"I-I can't." I turned around. "I just need to be away from you."

I darted to the other side of the courtyard and tried to quell the panic overwhelming me. What had just happened?

I gagged and struggled to slow my pulsating gills. Surely he hadn't just killed someone.

The courtyard closed in on me, and I tried to focus on a bright red anemone to steady myself. *Would he hurt me?*

And then I realized it didn't matter. Not after what he'd done.

"Jade." He came up behind me. "If you'd just—"

"We're done." My voice raised in pitch. "I don't want to see you again. Ever."

"Love, be reasonable." He laid his hand on my shoulder. "We're getting married."

"Don't touch me!" I hissed, darting forward.

He lurched toward me, spun me around, and pulled me toward him, his fingers digging into my forearm. "Jade, the naiads have taken so much from your family already. Don't let them take this."

"Father's death was an accident." *How dare he?* I wrenched my arm from his grasp.

"Was it?" He locked eyes with me.

I clenched my shaking hands to still them. "I don't know. I can't . . . just shut up and go away." My gills fluttered uncontrollably, and my heart pounded.

"You won't go to the inspectors?" he asked.

"That's all you care about?"

He didn't say anything, but his jaw tightened.

I turned and fled into the house, past Rhea's flirtations and Yvonna's smile, and out into the canal, where I came face-to-face with my mother.

"Jade, what's the matter?" Mother asked. "You look like you've seen a harpy."

My gills flared, and I reached for her arm to steady myself. "We have to go home. Right now."

"Jade, what—"

"We have to leave!" I yelled.

She stared at me. "If I don't go to the party, Yvonna will see it as a slight."

"I don't care."

"Alright." She took a long look at me. "Did you and Tor have a fight?"

"I don't ever want to see his face again."

She scoffed. "Don't be foolish."

"Mother, *please*." My voice trembled.

Her perceptive brown eyes searched mine. "Well, I suppose that is your right. Though I do hope you have a good reason. An engagement is not something to be ended on a whim."

I glanced down at my ring and pulled it off my finger. "Can you return this to Yvonna?"

She closed my fingers around the ring. "Take a day."

I shook my head and whispered, "He killed a naiad."

Her eyes widened. "What did you see?" She drew me into a comforting embrace. "What happened?"

I glanced back at Yvonna and Felix's house and murmured, "Home."

She nodded, and we turned around and began the short swim home, passing several other nobles who were dressed for the party. They gawked at me as they swam by, but Mother waved them off with a huff.

When we entered the refuge of our coral house, she turned to face me. "Start from the beginning."

I sucked water through my gills with a slow, shuddering groan. "Tor killed a naiad girl. I saw her body."

"Did you see him kill her?"

I shook my head. "But he admitted to it. Said he was trying to scare her. He thought I wouldn't care because of what happened to Father." I gripped the edge of the table. "I'm going to throw up."

Mother ran a hand over her face and swam over to gaze out the window at the canal. "This is grave. It could destabilize everything we've worked for over the last ten years. The king won't convict Tor over the death of a naiad servant. He can't. And when he doesn't, the naiads will riot in the canals. And after all the disappearances, too." She rubbed her temples. "I'm so sorry, my dear. I'll return the ring to Yvonna."

"We have to tell the inspectors. He can't just—"

"I'll see that King Stephanos knows of his indiscretion. He'll be quietly demoted and sent on patrol in the far reaches, near the deep ocean, for the remainder of his time of service. I'll make sure his career is over. He would have become High General, you know."

"He *murdered* her!" I screeched.

A gentle *whoosh* sounded to my left. I turned my head and saw my younger brother Benjamin frozen at the bottom of the vertical corridor. I tried to still my trembling chin to smile at him, but I couldn't control my face.

"Wait, *what* happened?" he demanded.

"Come here, urchin," I said, holding out my arms. He threw himself into my hug. "Everything's alright. Tor and I aren't getting married anymore, but you and Mother and I are just fine."

His back stiffened. "What did Tor do?"

I wasn't sure what to say.

Mother sighed. "He killed a naiad."

I winced but reminded myself that Benjamin wasn't a little kid anymore. He deserved to know.

She turned to me. "We can't bring the naiad back."

"But justice—"

"Is a great ideal. We live in the real world."

Benjamin looked from Mother to me. "You can't say that. If he killed someone, he has to go to trial."

"I'm sorry about the naiad," she said, "but I'm more concerned about the future of the other two thousand naiads in this city who will all be at risk if this gets out."

I couldn't believe my ears. I threw my engagement ring at the wall, and it sank to the floor. With a strangled sob, I darted out the door and into the canal.

Five minutes later, I arrived at Aunt Junia's house.

"Aunt Junia? It's me." I pounded on the door.

Aunt Junia—a short, heavyset mermaid who shared Mother's cerulean hair and brown eyes—opened the door and, with one look at me, guided me inside. "What's wrong?" she asked, her eyebrows furrowed.

Sobbing, I poured out the whole story.

She pulled me into a tight hug and shook her head. "You poor girl. And right after the engagement." She drew back to look me in the eye. "My sister's a good woman. The best of women. But today she's wrong."

I nodded, biting my lip. "I-I'm afraid Mother isn't turning him in because she's angry with the naiads about Father's—"

"Don't say it. It isn't true. Your mother has done more than anyone else in this city to protect the naiads over the last three years. You're absolutely sure Tor killed the poor thing?"

"Yes."

I stared at my hands. A horrible thought seized my mind, and I tried to suppress the shiver that ran down my body. "The missing naiads. At least four in the last six months. You don't think Tor could be . . ."

Her eyes widened. "I can't imagine," she murmured. A

long pause stretched between us. "But you never know," she said finally, a distant look in her eyes.

My lips tightened, and I stared up at the ceiling, focusing my gaze on the bioluminaries that bathed the small parlor in a gentle light. "If he's killing them, I . . . I couldn't live with myself if I didn't go to the inspectors."

"Well, then, there's only one thing to do." She nodded at me. "Maybe my sister is right. Maybe the courts will fail to convict, and the naiads will riot. It's still not our place to cover it up. Even if this girl is the only one he's killed. Throw the consequences to the depths." Magma bubbled in her eyes.

My spine tingled.

"Now, let's hurry," she said. "These things are time sensitive. He'll probably try to hide the body. The inspectors will call it another disappearance if they can't recover her."

She grabbed my hand and pulled me into the canal. We took a right and swam as quickly as we could in the direction of the inspectors' office, which lay near the king's palace at the center of the city.

In the background, the palace's pink and turquoise coral spiraled almost to the surface of the water. The sight always took my breath away, but in my distress, I hardly noticed it.

A friendly stingray descended into the city and hovered in the water in front of me, but all I could see was the naiad's face. She'd looked somehow familiar.

I shook it off. It didn't matter. Not yet.

Sooner than I'd imagined possible, we arrived at the inspectors' office. Aunt Junia hesitated on the threshold. "Jade?"

"Yes?"

"Don't tell them your mother didn't want to report Tor. The mer and the naiads have coexisted so uneasily, and I believe she doesn't want to upset that balance. Her intentions are good."

I nodded.

After another moment, Aunt Junia pushed open the door and swam into the small, dim room on the other side. Just being there brought my grief for Father crashing down on me. I closed my eyes to steady my nerves and then followed her. The room hadn't changed in three years—plain, gray walls uncluttered by even a hint of decoration, a functional table on the left-hand side topped by three clean stone tablets for note-taking, and a corridor that led to a set of back rooms.

"Excuse me?" Aunt Junia called out.

A slight current brushed against my skin just before a sallow, dark-haired merman emerged from the back of the corridor. He wore the crimson wrap and black sash of the inspectors.

"Can I help you?" he asked, his expression neutral.

Aunt Junia looked at me.

My voice sounded hollow as I said, "I'm here to report a murder."

CHAPTER

# THREE

The inspector's hand jerked as he reached for a stone tablet and a graphite scrib to write with. "I see. Victim?"

"I-I don't know. A naiad. Red hair. Probably a servant."

"Any ideas about the perpetrator?" His jaw twitched.

"Captain Tor of the Royal Mer Guard."

He dropped his scrib, and it sank to the floor. "That is quite an allegation. You are certain?"

I nodded.

He pursed his lips. "And you are?"

I furrowed my brow. "My name's Jade. I'm—I *was* engaged to Captain Tor."

"Ah."

I fidgeted as he paused, staring at me.

"You're sure that Captain Tor committed a murder?" he asked. "No action will be taken against you if you were to realize now that you'd misremembered. But I must warn you, his family is powerful. If this turns out to be a petty lover's squabble, I—"

"Excuse me?" Aunt Junia's eyes smoldered as she thrashed her fin against the floor. "Jade is the daughter of Advisor Cleo and a mermaid of excellent character. Do not impugn a lady of the court so casually, *sir*."

He lowered his gaze. "I beg your pardon, ladies. But I must ask again: You are certain?"

"Yes," I whispered.

"Where did this take place?" He stooped down to pick up the scrib and resumed scrawling on the tablet.

"I came upon him and the body in the courtyard of his parents' home."

He continued to jot down notes.

"He called it an accident," I said. "He asked me not to go to the inspectors."

"So you didn't see the murder?"

"No."

"I'm going to need you to describe your conversation with Captain Tor in greater detail." He trained his cold, slate-gray eyes on me.

I stumbled through the rest of the interview. By the time we concluded, numbness reached all the way down to my fin, like I had sunk to the darkest depths of the ocean beyond the breakwater.

I tried to chase away the memories of the last time the inspectors had interviewed me in that room. That time, I'd been with my mother, and I still couldn't quite believe my father was gone.

My gills flared as Aunt Junia and I swept out of the office and into the canal.

"I'm sorry that was so hard," Aunt Junia said. "It was the right thing to do. I'm proud of you."

"Is it worth it?" I asked. "Wrecking Tor's life? He's right. She *was* just a naiad."

"Shh. Don't say that. You've lost a lot, my dear. We all have. But if we give in to naked hate, we're no better than the liberationists who killed him."

I caught myself shivering. "I know. That's what Mother always says, too."

*Maybe someday I'll believe it.*

"Besides," Aunt Junia said, "your father's death might have been an accident." Her voice fell flat.

*An accident.* That had been the official line handed down by my mother and the king, but everyone knew better.

As we drifted back toward my home, one question weighed on me. "What will we tell Mother?"

"The truth."

"She'll be angry," I said.

"She'll be uneasy. There's a difference." She winced and rubbed her wrist.

"Are you alright?"

She nodded. "Aches and pains. Just wait twenty-five years for your turn."

We turned down another canal, past a school of silver fish and into the upper-class neighborhood I called home. Far too soon for my liking, we approached the house—one of the smallest and simplest on the canal—that I shared with my mother and brother.

"I'll come in with you," Aunt Junia said. "Just in case you need backup."

I pushed water through my gills. *I don't have the energy for a fight.* When I opened the door, the house lay quiet. "Mother?" I said.

We found Mother sitting in one of the woven hammocks around the dining room table, her tail and fin tucked underneath her. She looked up at Aunt Junia and me with a bone-weary smile. "I thought you two might be together."

I gazed at her as she set down a small webbed-foot dragon sculpture. Father had given it to her for her birthday the year before he died.

"You went to the inspectors, then?" she asked.

"Yes," I said. "I'm sorry."

She sighed. "Me too. I hope I'm wrong. I hope the courts do convict him. I think."

Worry lines radiated from her eyes. She hadn't looked this exhausted since the months following Father's death.

I hesitated. "I hope it doesn't become too much of a

public embarrassment for you. We're associated with his family because of the engagement, and a lot of the mer will think I shouldn't have turned him in. I don't want this to taint your career."

"There's nothing to be done about it now, and those sorts of considerations shouldn't matter. Besides, I'm in the king's good graces." She made eye contact with Aunt Junia, and something—I wasn't sure what—passed between them. "Our family can weather any current."

"Thank you," I whispered.

"Get some sleep, dear." Aunt Junia reached out and squeezed my arm. "I suspect tomorrow will be a difficult day."

Relieved, I darted up the corridor to my room without a backward glance at either of them.

I closed the seaweed screen that separated my room from the hallway and removed my wrap with painstaking precision. I doubted I'd ever wear it again, but I hung it up carefully all the same.

Reaching for my thin sleeping wrap, I struggled to quiet my thoughts. *In one evening, everything is different. Again.*

AFTER AN uneasy sleep plagued by nightmares, I woke up to yelling.

Disoriented, I stretched out quietly and listened. The commotion emanated from the first level of the house. After a moment, I recognized Yvonna's voice.

"Do you have any idea what kind of scandal your *tramp* of a daughter has brought down on all of us?" she screeched.

Mother's voice was as hard as steel. "You *will* apologize, madam, for such a characterization of my daughter, who is not the guilty party here. The last time I spoke with the king, murder was anathema in Thessalonike."

I edged toward my door. When I poked my head through the seaweed privacy screen, I found myself face-to-face with Benjamin. I reached out and grasped his hand.

"It's okay," I mouthed.

He squeezed my fingers.

"A naiad servant girl is worth ruining all our lives?" Yvonna screamed from below us. "That's skub, and you know it."

"I'll have you thrown out of my house if you continue to float here and insult me and my daughter. I returned the ring. We're no longer bound together as family. Go in peace."

"The depths we aren't," thundered a baritone voice.

*Felix.* I liked Tor's father even less than his mother.

"The marriage will go forward as planned. Jade will go to the inspectors today, recant her story, and have Tor released."

Mother scoffed. "Or what?"

Felix spoke again, his voice quieter. I strained to hear but couldn't make out his words.

Mother's voice rang out, startling me. "I would like to see you try. Leave my home immediately, or you will answer to the king."

Yvonna and Felix harrumphed and uttered another muffled threat, then all fell silent.

*They must've left.* "Are you okay?" I whispered to Benjamin.

"Mother has it under control," he murmured.

"I think they're gone now. I'm going down to talk to Mother, okay? I don't think she wanted you to hear any of that."

He nodded and swam back into his chamber. I cautiously drifted to the first level of the house.

"Mother?"

The front door stood open to allow the free flow of water through the house. Only the privacy screen blocked the view into the canal. No sign remained of my former in-laws.

Mother turned toward me. "They woke you?"

"Will everything be alright?"

"They can't follow through on their threats. I have the ear of the king."

"Desperate people are dangerous." I bit my thumbnail.

"Our position is secure."

I wished I had her confidence. The king respected her opinion, but Tor was beloved by the city, and Yvonna carried influence among the nobles. Maybe Mother was just trying to soothe me the way I soothed Benjamin.

Mother glanced at the tide glass. "It's nearly high tide. Pippa should've been here by now with my wrap that needed mending."

I couldn't focus on anything so banal. "So, Tor has been arrested?"

Mother nodded. "They found the naiad's body, and you are a witness. The crown accuses him."

"And the engagement is officially broken?"

"I am pleased to say that it is."

I fiddled with my empty ring finger. "I'm going to go for a swim with Kiki."

Mother's forehead wrinkled. "Don't go out alone until all this settles down."

"I can't just float here all day doing nothing. It'll drive me mad."

"I'll send for Rhea and Kora. I'm sure they can spare the day to keep you company. I must discuss the situation with the king today, of course."

I closed my eyes, overwhelmed by a vision of the red-haired naiad. When I opened them again, Mother was looking at me with a frown.

A familiar, dark-haired merman swam through the door. "Lady Cleo, Miss Jade."

"George!" I said, the tension in my shoulders releasing. He'd been our butler since before I was born. "You've heard."

He approached me and took hold of my hands. "I hope you're alright, Miss Jade."

I looked down at the floor with a shrug. "Not really, but I'm unharmed. Physically, anyway."

"If I may be so bold . . ." He looked from me to my mother.

"You know you may always speak your mind to us," Mother said.

"Were you aware of the identity of the young lady who died?"

I shook my head. "No, do you know?"

"I'm afraid it was Pippa's sister, Anna. Pippa sent word to ask for a few extra days to complete your mending, Lady Cleo."

I envisioned the naiad and Tor again. *That must've been why she looked so familiar.*

Mother's hand flew to her mouth. "Oh, the poor thing. She can have as long as she needs. I can make do with my other wraps."

"I told her the same thing, milady."

"And we'll send her a little money to help," she added. "I'm sure she'll lose some business over this if word of the connection gets out. Can you see that she receives an extra month's wages?"

"Of course."

"And invite Lady Rhea and Lady Kora to come see Jade today."

He bowed.

"As soon as you've returned," Mother continued, "I'll go speak to the king. I don't want Jade alone today. This news may provoke unrest in the city."

"Benjamin's here," I said.

"I'd like myself or George or your Aunt Junia to be here, too," she replied. "Peace is fragile, and my children are precious to me." She turned toward George. "That's all. Go in peace."

"Peace be upon you." He pressed his right fist against his heart, turned, and swam out of the house and into the busy canal.

Mother looked at me. "Go get dressed so you can entertain your guests." Glancing at the privacy curtain separating us from the canal, she said, "Close and lock the door on the way up."

She reached for a stone tablet and a scrib and began to jot down notes. I didn't ask what she was writing.

I shut the door and fastened the lock, then turned to float up the vertical corridor and down the hall to my room. With a heavy sigh, I sank into the chair in front of my mirror to await my friends' arrival.

A few minutes later, I heard the gentle *swish* of my curtain.

"Jade?" a soft voice called.

I turned to see a young mermaid with long, turquoise hair and soft brown eyes. "Oh, Kora. I'm so glad you're here."

Kora pulled me into an embrace. "I'm so, so sorry about everything that's happened. I can't imagine how you must be feeling."

"It's more shocking than anything, really. I didn't know Tor all that well. It wasn't like we got engaged out of irrepressible love or any of that nonsense."

"No," she said with a chuckle, "but you cared about him."

I ran my thumb over my ring finger. "Well, none of that matters now," I said, willing my voice to stay steady.

She hesitated. "The gossip floating around the city says that you turned him in."

"It's true." I turned to stare out the window at the nearly empty canal.

"Wow. I'm surprised, I guess."

"I saw it. The aftermath."

She squeezed my hand. "I'm so sorry, dear."

"Jaaaaade!" Rhea wailed from the first floor of the house. A moment later, she darted through the curtain. "Are you alright? Has Tor really been arrested? Is that why you left so early? What's going on?"

Her dark hair ballooned around her face as she threw back her head and came to an abrupt halt. She grabbed my arm.

I tried to smile at her, but I'm pretty sure it looked like a grimace. "Tor killed a naiad. He's been arrested, and the crown accuses him. The engagement is over." My awful suspicion about the missing naiads floated through my mind, but I kept it to myself.

Her hand flew to her mouth. "I can't believe it."

Kora shifted and sank down to sit on the floor, one hand on the ground and the other wrapped around her amber tail. "This is going to be a pretty big scandal, isn't it?"

I sighed. "There isn't any way around it. Mother is concerned that the courts won't convict and the naiads will riot. Yvonna has pledged to destroy us if I don't recant the story."

"If you don't recant the story?" Rhea asked, her lips quirked.

Kora shot her a sharp look. "Don't," she mouthed.

"It's okay," I said, turning to Rhea. "I stumbled on it right after it happened. I reported it to the inspectors."

Rhea shrieked and began babbling incoherently. Maybe I could have understood her if I'd tried, but I felt too tired to heed her emotional breakdown. I was too close to one of my own.

"Why don't we get some open water?" I asked. "Let's all go for a swim with Kiki."

Rhea fell silent, but her eyes stayed wide open.

"I think that's a great idea," said Kora.

Rhea nodded, so I ran a comb through my hair and drifted through my curtain and down the corridor to the front door. Kora and Rhea followed close behind.

As we hastened down the canal, my skin prickled. *Is it just my imagination, or are people staring at me?*

"Jade?" Kora whispered. "Let's hurry."

*So it's not my imagination.*

We swam faster, only relaxing when we zipped through the entrance to the city, past the guards, and out onto the reef. I didn't dare meet the gazes of Tor's compatriots.

"Kiki?" I called as we made our way to the section of reef where she often lingered, past vermillion anemone and the long, waving black tendrils of a field of seagrass.

I heard clicking and knew she was nearby. A moment later, a streak of gray sailed toward us from above, skimming the surface where the ocean kissed the air.

"Kiki!" I rubbed her belly as she dove down and greeted me. "Let's go," I called to Rhea and Kora.

We swam alongside Kiki and surged toward the open water on the other side of the drop-off like we'd done so many times as kids. For a moment, I wished I'd come alone so I could ride Kiki—even a dolphin couldn't tow three fully grown mermaids at once. But when I saw the gleeful grin on Kora's face, I was glad I'd brought my friends out. It had been a while since I'd shared Kiki.

"Do you want to talk about it?" Kora asked.

My gills flared. "I don't know." I closed my eyes for a moment, and when I opened them again, I recounted the conversation I'd had with Tor.

When I finished, Kora squeezed my hand. Rhea didn't say anything, and I thanked the tides that she'd calmed down.

As we soared through the open water, above the dark depths of the ocean that our parents had warned us never to flirt with, I gloried in the uninhibited freedom of life away from the city. Here, with only Kiki and my friends, no one cared that I was supposed to be proper and safe. Here, I could just be.

I tried to quell my sense of longing. Dwelling on my desire for simplicity and solitude wouldn't do me any good in the long term. Given my position, I had to be responsible.

There was no way around it. Just like I couldn't avoid turning Tor in.

"I miss him already, but I'm glad the engagement is over," I said to no one in particular.

"Why are you glad?" Kora cocked her head, and her turquoise hair streamed out behind her.

"Because now I know he can get violent if he feels threatened. I'm sorry about the girl that died, but if it had to happen, at least it let me see this side of him before I married him."

"I don't know," Rhea said. "You've lost out on a great opportunity, I think."

Kora and I gaped at each other but didn't say anything.

"I'm serious. He's a good guy," Rhea said. "On the whole."

"Seriously?" Kora interjected. "I know he's rich and beautiful, but he killed someone."

"Jade said he was trying to protect his family. That counts for something."

"It doesn't justify murder," said Kora.

"We don't *know* it was murder. He claimed he wasn't trying to kill the girl."

"He attacked her, and she died," I said, my voice flat. "Sounds like murder to me."

Rhea shrugged. "Well, if I ever have a son, I hope he's loyal to our family above everything." Then she grabbed my hand, her fingernails digging into my skin.

I scanned the water to see what had startled her and chuckled. A shark, no longer than my tail, swam alongside us.

"Well, hello there, little one," I said, reaching over to scratch its neck.

Kora looked at me dubiously.

"It's tiny," I said. "Besides, if it were going to get aggressive, it would have done so already."

Shaking her head, Kora said, "You always did have the strangest way with wild animals."

"Oh, I'm strange am I?" I grinned at her.

"In a good way. I always thought it was kind of cool."

Rhea's eyes bulged as the shark brushed against her. "I want to go home," she said, her voice an octave higher than normal.

I rolled my eyes but didn't argue. *This is why I don't share Kiki with them anymore.*

We turned to swim back toward the reef and Thessalonike. Rhea's shoulders visibly relaxed when we crossed the breakwater back into the warm shallows.

I glanced behind us, and the little shark was gone. A pang of disappointment pricked my stomach. I'd thought it was pretty cute.

We drew close to the coral walls of Thessalonike, and Kiki took that as her cue to leave. She nudged my arm with her nose and darted away.

*Perhaps she sees a fish she wants to chase.*

I didn't really know why I always made excuses. Kiki hated the city, and she always got nervous when she saw domesticated dolphins. I didn't blame her. I wouldn't want to live in Thessalonike as a dolphin.

Sometimes I didn't even want to live there as a mermaid.

My friends and I swam to the entrance of the city, and this time I had no choice but to make eye contact with the guards.

My heart plummeted. The commanding officer was Maximus, Tor's best friend. His deep blue eyes met mine, and I couldn't figure out what emotions swirled in them.

"I'm sorry," I said.

He broke eye contact. "You may pass."

One of his underlings, a merman I didn't recognize, sneered at me as we swam by. "I hope you're satisfied, tramp. And your little harpy friends, too."

CHAPTER

# FOUR

"Sergeant!" barked Maximus.

The merman who had harassed us turned to look at his leader. "Aye, sir?"

"Apologize to Lady Jade, and I'll pretend I didn't hear you insult Cleo's daughter."

The sergeant's jaw tightened. I didn't look at him as he mumbled an apology.

"Thanks," I murmured. I grabbed Rhea's arm and bolted into the city. Once out of earshot, I said, "I guess everyone's heard."

We attracted more stares as we swam back toward my house. As we passed into the first circle of the city, I caught a glimpse of Adella, one of my mother's friends. I waved at her, but she just glanced at me and turned away.

*Scandal travels fast.*

Kora and Rhea both noticed.

"Don't worry." Kora looped her arm around my shoulder. "They did the same thing to Aphra last year when she got pregnant, but everything's fine now that the baby's here."

"But I didn't *do* anything," I hissed.

"You know how it is," said Kora. "Tainted by association. And some of them probably think you shouldn't have gone to the inspectors over a naiad."

Rhea hadn't said anything for several minutes, which was decidedly un-Rhea-like.

We turned onto my canal and quickly swept inside my house to avoid the cold demeanor of the other nobles—and even a few of the merchants.

"You made a mistake," Rhea said once we reached the safety of my home. "Tor is popular, and his family's powerful."

"What else was I supposed to do?" I demanded.

Rhea shrugged, halting on the far side of the room. "Do you think for a moment that Yvonna hasn't spent the whole day assassinating your character and spreading stories that you made the whole thing up because you were mad or jealous? She's probably even saying you killed the naiad yourself or something."

My hands trembled, and I looked at Kora. She was staring at the floor.

"They'd be crazy to believe that," I said.

"Jade?" Kora said, her voice small.

I closed my eyes. "What is it?"

"I—my family. We're not like yours. My parents don't wield the kind of power or influence with the king that your mother does. We haven't ranked among the nobility for very long."

*Tainted by association.*

"You know my position isn't safe," she continued. "To secure an elite career, I need to marry someone who—"

"I get it," I said, rubbing the back of my neck.

"No—" Her face crumpled. "—it's not like that. I still want to see you. I just . . . not out in public for now. And I can't come here."

I raised an eyebrow. "So you'll be my friend, you just won't swim at my side or risk *associating* with me?"

"You're being unfair," snapped Rhea. "For you and your family, this *will* wash away. Kora has no guarantees. If Yvonna set her mind to it—"

"I get it!" I yelled.

We floated in uncomfortable silence.

"You can go now," I said. "Both of you."

"Please come see me soon," said Kora, grabbing my hand. "Just . . . I know it sounds awful, but if you could cloak yourself until you get inside my house . . ."

"I said you can go," I whispered.

I didn't turn to watch as they swam out the door.

"ARE YOU ALRIGHT?" George's voice startled me from my miserable reverie.

I looked up at him with a half-smile. "Yeah. Funny how everything can change at once, you know?"

"You did the right thing," he said. "Even if your friends can't see it. Here, come sit down."

He led me to the table and helped me into the hammock, then he moved to the other side of the table and reached toward me, wrapping my hands in his.

"Everything changed for Pippa yesterday, too, and she wouldn't have ever known what happened if you hadn't gone to the inspectors. None of this is your fault. In fact, you're starting to set things right. As right as they can be, anyway."

*Pippa.* A twinge of guilt curled in my stomach. I'd hardly thought about how she must be feeling.

That kind of grief had eviscerated me—waves of sorrow that couldn't be assuaged but that, with no warning, gave way to debilitating numbness so profound it left me wondering if I, rather than Father, had really died that day. And then a sight or sound would trigger another swell of pain and plunge me back into the soul-tearing horror of it all.

*Yes. Pippa. I should talk to her.*

"Thanks, George," I said.

"And yes," he said, "you should go see Pippa."

I stared at him. "How did you—"

"I've known you since the day you were born. You can't hide your thoughts from me." He winked and ruffled my hair before pushing away from the table and gliding out of my room and down the first-level hall toward the parlor.

I smiled. *Dependable, perceptive George!* It seemed like he always knew the right thing to say.

But then, the worry hit me.

*The naiad quarter?*

I'd never been to that part of the city before. It was a dangerous place, and if I was honest with myself, I didn't really know how to interact with naiads. Not in that way, anyway.

*I mean, yes, we've had naiad servants. But interacting with a servant is simple. You tell them what to do, they do it, and you thank them.* I'd always prided myself on treating servants—mer or naiad—with respect. *But to bring condolences to Pippa? Will I know what to say?*

I glanced at the tide glass and then out the window. If I meant to visit Pippa tonight, I'd need to go soon.

I shook my head. *Better to go in two or three days and give her a little more time to work through the numb disbelief.*

How well I remembered the numb disbelief. I would go in the morning in two days, I decided.

And in the meantime, I wouldn't go anywhere else.

BENJAMIN ARRIVED home from school that day with a vacant expression on his face.

"What's wrong, urchin?" I hugged him. "They didn't give you a hard time about Tor and me, did they?"

"It's not your fault," he said.

I felt like someone had punched me in the stomach, but I

managed a winning smile. "Who was mean to you? I'll throw them to a school of sharks."

He laughed and rolled his eyes. "Really, it's fine. They just like to talk. That's all."

"I've had quite a day myself."

"Sounds like *I* might need to throw someone to the sharks."

I curled my arm around his shoulder and ruffled his short but perfectly coiffed blue hair. "That's why you're my favorite."

"Hey," he said, quirking his lips as he smoothed his hair back into place.

"Seriously, though." I pulled back and crossed my arms. "We're gonna get through this together. The whole family. And if anyone gives you a hard time, I'll beat 'em up."

He stared into the distance. "Do you think Pippa's doing alright?"

"No." I toyed with a thread that had come loose at the edge of my wrap. "I'm sure she isn't. I mean, you remember how it was when Father died."

"I dealt with it differently than you did. It didn't seem real to me for the longest time."

"And when it hit you?"

He paused. "Yeah, I guess Pippa's probably pretty bad off right now."

"I'm going to see her in a couple days. She'll appreciate your concern."

He smiled, but it didn't quite reach his eyes. "Are you afraid?" he finally asked. "About all of this?"

"You've grown up a lot when I wasn't looking."

"You're avoiding the question."

I sighed. "Yeah. I'm a little afraid and a lot sad. Yesterday morning I was planning a wedding. When I came in from the reef, I caught myself wondering whether we should serve lobster or swordfish to the guests after the ceremony."

"I'm sorry."

"And I know you must be disappointed, too," I continued. "You admired Tor."

He snorted. "I don't admire him if he's killing people."

I burst out laughing. "No," I managed. "No, I don't suppose you do." My laughter turned to sobs, and Benjamin rested his hand on my shoulder. "It's just awful," I whispered. "Everything about this whole skub situation."

"Yeah. It is. I wish I could fix it, but since I can't, want a snack?"

"You know how to cheer me up," I said with a chuckle. Numbness still clenched at my heart, but it felt good to remember that I wasn't alone. "What do we have in the kitchen?"

TWO DAYS LATER, George provided me with Pippa's address, and I found myself donning a cloak and flitting toward the naiad quarter. Kora was right; it was easier to move around the city with my identity concealed.

My nerves fluttered as I soared through the sandy-bottomed canals and crossed the boundary between the part of Thessalonike that belonged to the mer and the section we had given to the naiads when they'd sought refuge with us ten years earlier.

Even though my identity was hidden, I couldn't conceal that I was mer, and I caught several curious glances from naiads as they jetted through the water on currents of bubbles.

It wasn't that mer never came to this part of the city—I saw two others on my way to Pippa's—so I wondered why I was attracting so much attention. They couldn't know I was Tor's fiancée.

*Ex-fiancée*, I reminded myself. Something like grief took hold of me, but I shook it off and swam faster to try to distract myself.

More naiads turned to look at me as I hastened through the quarter. Pulling my cloak tighter around my face, I counted the canals I passed until I found Pippa's.

I blinked several times in succession at the small, worn homes chiseled out of rock. They probably consisted of only one room each. Barnacles clung to the exteriors, and tan sandstone—rather than the brilliant coral I was accustomed to—made up the walls.

Not that I'd expected the naiads to live like the nobles. When I thought about it, I wasn't sure *what* I'd expected.

I hesitated in front of Pippa's house and rapped on the door three times. After a long, agonizing moment, she opened the door. Her bloodshot eyes widened. "Lady Jade? How can I help you?"

"I've brought you a mourning gift," I said, holding out an elegant sapphire necklace that I secretly hated. "And I thought you might like some company."

"Oh. Of course," she said, taking the necklace from my hand and glancing at it with a wry expression. "Come in. It isn't much."

I followed her inside and tried not to let my astonishment show. How could two people live in such close quarters?

*Not that it matters anymore*, I thought grimly. *Only one person lives here now.*

I cleared my throat. "I'm very sorry about your sister," I said, sinking into one of the fishing-net hammocks that lined her rough-hewn table.

"From what I understand, you discovered her?" she asked, her voice quavering. She set the necklace on the table and smoothed her flowing dress.

"Yes."

She ran a hand through her long, chestnut locks. "I'm sorry you had to see that."

My throat tightened. "Yes," I said, desperately searching for something to say. "You saw us after Father died, so you know that I have some understanding of—"

"Stop." Pippa held up her hand. "It was kind of you to come here today, but you don't understand."

"I—"

"Lady Jade, with all due respect, I'm sure you grieved when your father died, but you are among your people. You have family and friends and enough money to get by even if all your connections are stripped away. My family is dead. All of them. My parents died when the poison began to course through the rivers, and my brother was killed by a hydra during the journey to Thessalonike.

"And this promised land? Where we were assured we would be welcome because of our longstanding trade relationship with the mer? We live in poverty. We are harassed. We are hated. They're afraid of our water-casting. And now Anna is gone, along with her income, which helped pay the rent for this house. No, Lady Jade, you do not understand."

I opened my mouth and then closed it again. *I cannot imagine.*

"I'm sorry," she said. "You mean well. I overstepped."

"No." I threaded my fingers together. "I was insensitive."

She chuckled quietly, scratching her neck. "It's been a difficult week. I still half-expect her to burst through the door at any moment."

"Let's start over," I said. "I'm very sorry to hear about Anna. Do you want to talk about her?"

A wistful smile played on her lips. "What can I say? She was my baby sister. Headstrong, annoying, beautiful." Her voice cracked.

I remained silent and imagined how I'd feel if someone

hurt Benjamin. I marveled at her composure. In her place, I'd hunt down Tor and kill him myself.

"She worked hard. She'd grown up so much in the last couple of years. What was your father like?"

I glanced up, startled. "Well, he was a really good person. A huge help to my mother but successful in his own right. So perceptive it frustrated me. Now I miss his ability to pinpoint what was going on at any given time. He was a lot like George, actually. They always got along. They were friends, despite their difference in rank."

*I'm rambling now*, I realized. I fell quiet.

A soft smile played on her lips. "Perhaps you do understand, just a little."

I met her gaze, and we both relaxed. "What did you and Anna do together?"

"Well, recently we worked a lot." She crossed her legs underneath her billowy dress. "The owner raised our rent two months ago, and we couldn't really afford it anymore."

I arched an eyebrow but couldn't think of anything to say that wouldn't sound like an insult.

"When we were younger, we liked to cross the breakwater and swim over the deep ocean."

"No way!" I leaned forward. "My dolphin and I do that all the time."

Her eyes lit up. "I've never heard of a mer who voluntarily left the safety of the reef to swim over the drop-off."

"I know. My friends think I'm crazy. I used to go with them when we were small, but they've grown afraid like everyone else. I know it's a risk, but I figure as long as I have Kiki with me, it'll be alright."

"How'd you end up with a dolphin?"

"She was orphaned by a webbed-foot dragon when I was eleven. One of the very first times my parents let me leave the city alone, I saw her mother get dragged off the reef. Have you ever heard a dolphin scream before?"

She shook her head.

"It's the most haunting thing you can imagine," I said. "Kiki was just swimming back and forth like she didn't know what to do. The whole pod must've been scared off. Even though I was nervous that the dragon might come back, I waited out there with her for three hours, but her pod never returned for her."

"I'm surprised she let you get close."

"She actually swam right up to me as soon as she saw me. It was like she knew I wanted to protect her."

"What'd you do when you realized she'd been left behind?"

Laughing, I said, "I brought her right past the guards into the city and hid her in my room for almost two months before Father caught me. I thought for sure he'd make me return her to the reef, but he said I could keep her until she was big enough to take care of herself. Mother took more convincing, but Father persuaded her. After she got too big to stay in my room, I took her back outside the city. She's stayed nearby ever since, so I go out to swim with her a few days a week."

Pippa's face lit up. "Anna would have loved that story. She would have wanted to meet Kiki."

"Well, I'll have to take you out to see her someday when you aren't working. We can swim in the deep water and pretend that Thessalonike and all its nonsense doesn't exist."

"Do you mean that?" Something like hope flickered in her eyes.

"Yes," I said, reaching across the table to grasp her hand. "You and I both feel alone in this city, I think."

"You lost a lot that day too, didn't you?"

"Hmm?"

"When Anna died. You threw away an engagement."

"I was engaged to a powerful merman with a violent

streak," I said, smoothing my fuchsia hair. "That's a nasty combination. It sucked, but I don't think I lost anything by giving him up. Although half the city seems to hate me now. I think his mother may literally be going from house to house spreading lies. And everyone loves him, so they want to believe her." I stared at the dull sandstone wall.

"His mother's a harpy."

"You do the mending for them?"

She held her hands in front of her and cast a stream of water from fingertip to fingertip. "No, but Anna worked in their house. She was always coming home with stories about how Yvonna had been awful to her."

"Somehow that doesn't surprise me," I said. "She seems sharp with anyone from a lower social strata. Maybe that's why she's always made me uncomfortable."

"I mean, she's not a monster. The family paid Anna fairly. They offered better wages than almost any of the mer, in fact. And even though Yvonna got shrill, she never hit Anna or threatened to fire her, like a lot of our friends' employers." She sighed. "I don't know. Anna was always frustrated, but it was a good job."

"Well, regardless, Yvonna's angry, and she's powerful, so that makes her dangerous to all of us. We'll just have to be careful for a while."

"Thanks for going up against them. I don't know that I would've been that brave in your place."

I shrugged. "It wasn't—"

Shouts from outside the house cut me off. Pippa and I looked at each other.

"What's going on?" I asked.

Then a tremor shook the house.

Pippa stood, and I darted upward.

A male voice called out, "Naiad scum!"

Pippa's lips tightened. "You need to get out of here," she whispered. "It's dangerous."

I wasn't sure I was the one in danger.

Another tremor. She grabbed my hand.

"Through here." She dragged me toward the back wall, moved a pile of rocks one by one, and exposed a door in the floor.

"What the—"

"Not now," she hissed as she opened the door and pushed me through it.

When my eyes adjusted, I found myself in a shadowed, horizontal corridor that seemed to run the length of the houses on the canal. The yells from above me grew louder. I heard a resounding *crack*.

"Pippa?" I whispered.

She jumped down beside me, a money pouch hanging around her neck, and then reached up to pull down the trapdoor. When it was secured, she started down the corridor, casting a gentle current behind us.

"Hurry," she said. "This won't hold them off for long."

We hastened down the corridor until we reached what I assumed to be the end of the canal.

"Up here," she said, unhooking another trapdoor and drifting upward.

With a flick of my fin, I followed her, and we broke out into the light. I hazarded a glance back in the direction of her house just in time to see a mob of about a dozen mer break down her door and stream inside.

"Depths, Pippa! Can—"

"I'll explain later," she said again. "We have to go. Out of the naiad quarter if at all possible."

I realized I'd left my cloak in her house in our rush.

"Sure," I said, hoping we wouldn't be noticed. "We can go to my house. No one will bother us there."

We surged forward. The last remaining merman on the canal turned toward us just before we rounded the corner and disappeared out of sight of the mob.

"Hey!" he yelled, recognizing either Pippa or me. I wasn't sure which.

"Swim." I darted forward as fast as my fin could propel me.

Pippa shaped a stream of water with her hands, creating a narrow but rapid current on which to push herself forward so she easily kept pace with me. We careened around a corner and onto a wide canal, sparsely populated by naiads.

But the mer in pursuit proved faster, and before we could reach the edge of the quarter, the fastest of them grabbed my fin and tugged me backward. Pain shot up my tail, all the way into my waist.

"What do you think you're doing with the naiads, *Lady* Jade?" the merman spat. "More conspiracies?"

Pippa shot a stream of water at him and knocked him backward. I scrambled away.

With a shout, he launched toward Pippa and grabbed ahold of her body. He delivered one punch to her side, and she doubled over. I screamed and darted forward to push him away from her, but another merman grabbed my arms and pinned them behind my back.

Pippa drew her hands back to pelt her assailant with another surge of water, but he grasped both her slender wrists in one of his hands. Then he yanked a small coral blade from his belt and plunged it into her side.

CHAPTER

# FIVE

The merman floated backward for a moment, surveyed the damage, and darted away.

I froze. Everything stopped.

Then Pippa sank toward the seafloor, a stream of dark red blood curling upward away from her body, and I rushed forward to catch her.

"Help!" I screamed. I looked desperately from house to house, but the canal was empty except for the mob now slowly backing away from us.

I caught a glimpse of a naiad peeking out from behind a curtain across the canal, but no one came to our aid.

Gathering Pippa up, I pressed my hand against her wound, lunged forward, and surged out of the quarter toward the house of physicians, praying I could get her there before it was too late. Blood leaked through my fingers, and I looked up toward the surface, on alert for sharks or dragons that might be drawn to the smell.

"Move!" I yelled at a dolphin driver blocking my way as I turned onto a busy canal. The house of physicians lay two blocks away.

The driver looked up at me and down at the blood seeping from Pippa's wound. His face blanched. He reached forward and slapped his dolphin's side, and they rushed away from us.

Murmurs spread through the crowd as I soared down the canal. I burst into the house of physicians.

A mermaid in a close-fitting, white wrap met my gaze. My hands trembled. "She's been stabbed."

I LOOPED up and down the corridor near Pippa's room. The physicians had assured me they were doing everything they could to control the bleeding and mend the damage, but it brought me no comfort.

*Did I bring the danger to her? Was I followed?*

Another white-clad mermaid approached me. "Lady Jade? You brought in the naiad, right? With the stab wound?"

I nodded, entwining my fingers. "She's a friend. How is she?"

"We're going to keep her for a few days to make sure infection doesn't set in, but she's very lucky you were there to bring her in. I think she's going to be just fine."

Relief swept over my tense body, and I pushed water through my gills. "Thank you. I'm very glad to hear that. Can I see her?"

"Sure," she said. "We're done working on her for now."

I followed her into a room with light blue coral walls. Pippa lay on a bed on the far side of the room.

"How are you holding up?" I asked.

A hint of a smile cracked her lips. "It's been a rough week."

I tilted my head. "It speaks well of you that you can still smile."

"I learned a long time ago that you have to be able to laugh no matter what. Otherwise you start weeping and never stop."

I squeezed her hand. "Is there anything my family can do for you?"

She shook her head, her lips tightening. "I'll be alright, Lady Jade."

"The physicians reported the attack to the inspectors, as the law requires." I rubbed my temples. "I've already described your attacker to them."

"Thank you."

"Pippa . . ." I trailed off, unsure how to continue. "I suspect your home was destroyed because I visited. I think it's possible—likely, even—that you would've been left alone if you hadn't been associated with me. The mer who are angry with me can't go after me directly. But when they saw me go to your house—"

"They came after me because I'm not so protected?"

I nodded.

"Lady Jade—"

"Jade will do. You've earned the right to drop my title."

"You don't have any idea—" She winced. "—what goes on in the naiad quarter, do you?"

I furrowed my eyebrows.

"These sorts of attacks aren't uncommon. They happen every week, it seems like."

I drew back. *Every week?*

"And honestly," she continued, "with everyone talking about Anna's death, I was expecting it."

"What—no. My mother has devoted her whole career to improving conditions in the quarter. I would know if—"

"Your mother does a lot of good for the naiads, but one bureaucrat, however well-intentioned, can't fix what's broken."

*One bureaucrat, my fin.* But I let it pass. "If we could just set the differences between our peoples aside, perhaps things could get better."

She bit her lip. "If you hadn't seen Anna's body with your own eyes, would you have believed that Tor killed her? Or would you have sided with him because the idea that he brutally attacked her seemed so preposterous?"

"I . . ."

Her voice softened. "And even if you believed him guilty, if you hadn't encountered firsthand the horror of his actions, would you be one of the voices in the canals murmuring that my sister had it coming to her? That surely she'd provoked him?"

"Well, she may have provoked him. He said she was extorting his family."

She shook her head. "See? It's not quite that simple, is it?"

I didn't know what to say. "I'm sorry," I finally managed.

"It's not your fault. None of it is," she said. "These are just realities we have to deal with."

"Can you and I be friends?" I asked, straightening my back. "In spite of it all, can we try, anyway?"

She smiled softly at me. "We both need a friend right now, I think."

*That's truer than you know.* "I should go soon, or Mother will send out a search party for me. But I'll come back and see you. Tomorrow if I can."

"Be careful on the canals. I'll understand if it's too dangerous for you to travel. I, of all people, know how uncertain everything is right now."

"When you're well enough to catch up on your mending, why don't you do it from our house during the day? That might be safer for you."

"I'll think about it," she said. "Thanks for your concern. Go in peace."

"And peace be upon you." I turned to leave. I ignored the stares of the physicians as I left the house of healing.

"JADE?" Mother called as I entered the house, her voice cracking with anxiety and anger.

"I'm here," I said. *This is going to be a fun conversation.*

Aunt Junia darted into the entryway. "We're so glad you're home. Your mother's been worried."

*No point in trying to keep it from them. Even if they don't know yet, they will soon.* "I assume you heard that I was in the naiad quarter when Pippa's house was attacked?"

"Mmm-hmm." Aunt Junia's tone suggested disapproval, but I detected a twinkle of pride in her eyes.

Mother floated around the corner, her eyes narrowed on me. "Were you trying to get yourself killed, going there?"

I decided that this wasn't the moment to mention that George had suggested I go. "I'm sorry. I wanted to offer my condolences to Pippa in person."

Mother ran her hands through her hair. "You don't help mer-naiad relations by putting yourself in that kind of danger. Not this week, especially. If you'd been killed, we'd be clashing in the canals."

"I'm sure the mer would love me a lot more if I *were* dead," I mumbled.

She shot me a sharp look. "As it is, some of the naiads have been restless. We've had a few situations."

"Situations?"

"Most recently a riot. Small. Easily contained. But the king is unhappy."

"An eruption of violence could destroy everything the king and his advisors have been working for—trying to ease the naiads into full participation in society," Aunt Junia said.

"Is it true that gangs of mer have been attacking naiad homes for years?" I asked.

Mother and Aunt Junia looked at each other.

Aunt Junia fingered the frayed edge of her wrap. "It's true. It's always been true."

"Then why doesn't anyone talk about it?"

"It's not conducive to promoting peace." Aunt Junia's gills flared.

I swished my tail back and forth. "Neither are home invasions. Or blade attacks."

"Sometimes we have to make short-term sacrifices for long-term gains," said Aunt Junia.

I raised an eyebrow. "That doesn't seem—"

"Pippa's attacker has already been found," said Mother. "His compatriots turned him in to the inspectors for violating the prohibition against blades."

"As they should have." Aunt Junia raised her eyebrows. "He could have brought a feeding frenzy of sharks on all of us with his actions."

"So he's to be expelled?" I asked.

Mother nodded. "The king has already declared the attack to be anathema. And Jade? Don't go back to the naiad quarter until everything calms down." Her voice hitched. "I can't lose you. Especially not after your father."

I looked down at the floor.

"Promise me, Jade."

I grunted at her and flitted up the corridor.

"*Jade.*"

"I can't have this conversation right now. I'm sorry," I called from the second level of the house. With a strangled sob, I burst through the kelp screen into my room. Floating in front of my window, I let my thoughts wander.

*What if I just left? I could pack a bag, leave the city, and swim off with Kiki. I'm of age. No one could stop me.*

I wondered what the canals of Marbella looked like and if I could blend into the crowd of commoners there.

*The Thessaloniken ambassador and his family would recognize me. But it's a big city . . .*

"Jade?" Benjamin's voice from the hallway pulled me back to reality. "Can I come in?"

My gills flared. "I need to be alone."

"Please? Just for a second."

"Fine."

He peeked through the kelp and floated into my room. "I'm sorry she flipped out on you."

"Me too."

"Is Pippa gonna be okay?"

"I'm surprised you heard about that." I sank onto my hammock.

"Psh. Don't be silly. I hear everything."

I gave him a sad smile. "That you do, urchin."

"Anyway, today I heard something that I thought you needed to know about."

I tried to keep my face calm. "What is it?"

He picked at his thumbnail. "You really need to be careful. Yvonna's out for blood."

I scoffed. "Of course she is. She's probably meeting with sleazy assassins in back canals."

"No, you don't understand. Not like that. Mariana says she saw Yvonna meeting with Andronicus."

I stared at him, quirking my eyebrow. "Andronicus who?"

He rolled his eyes. "You really need to get out more. Andronicus? Leader of the anti-monarchists?"

"I didn't realize the rabble had gotten so organized. What are they doing these days? Still trying to expel the naiads? Or . . . what was it? Protesting that tariff?"

He sat beside me on the hammock. "I think they're planning to overthrow the king."

CHAPTER

# SIX

"We hereby announce the dissolution of the engagement between Lady Jade Cleopola and Captain Tor Felicipolos," the crier called from our canal on his morning round.

I cringed.

"As a result of criminal proceedings in which the crown accuses Captain Tor of the murder of the naiad Anna Brook, a servant in the employ of Captain Tor's parents, Lady Yvonna Cassiapola and Lord Felix Andreapolos."

The crier's words reached me where I sat inside my room. To honor Mother's request—and, if I was being honest with myself, because the idea terrified me—I hadn't returned to the naiad quarter or gone back to the house of physicians in the days since my disastrous visit.

Two seahorses drifted through my window, and I smiled at them. "Hi, friends."

*Friends.*

Every time I thought of the conversation I'd had with Rhea and Kora, heat rose in my cheeks. *I still want to see you,* Kora had said. *Just . . . not out in public for now.*

I tried—and failed—to suppress the stab of pain that bloomed in my chest. *It isn't Kora's fault. She's doing what she has to do to protect herself and her family. I have no idea what I'd do in her place.*

I said it over and over to myself, but it didn't comfort

me. Still, holding a grudge against my oldest and best friends wouldn't do anyone any good. I decided I'd visit Kora at her home.

*Surely Mother wouldn't object to that. It's not like she expects me to stay indoors like a prisoner. And even if she does, I'm not a child anymore.*

I searched out my most nondescript black wrap so I wouldn't draw attention to myself in the canals.

A timid knock sounded on the door below. "Lady Jade?" a soft voice called.

*Pippa.*

I heard the door open and George say, "Come in, my dear. Do you need anything to eat?"

"No, but thank you. It's kind of you to ask."

I swept down to the first level of the house and reached for Pippa's hand. "I'm so glad you came. How do you feel?"

"The wound still hurts, of course, but I can do most things as long as I don't walk too quickly." She glanced down. "Well, I can't cast water yet. But I should be able to by next week."

"I'm so glad to hear that," I said. "And how are you doing otherwise?"

Her face remained impassive. "As well as can be expected. I don't really want to talk about it if you don't mind."

George excused himself to the kitchen.

"Oh. Okay." I glanced at the basket in her hand. "Taking me up on my offer to work here during the day?"

"If it's still on the table," she said. "And I brought your cloak back. You left it when we fled. I hate to intrude, but it'll be a week before the doorway to my home is repaired, and I don't feel safe there." She handed me the cloak, and I caressed the fabric as I draped it over my arm.

"It's no intrusion." I wrinkled my nose. "Not for another week? Do you have somewhere to go at night?"

"I've been staying with a friend."

"Good," I said too quickly. We stared at each other for an awkward moment.

Pippa set down her basket.

"I was just on my way to visit my friend Kora," I said. "You don't mind being here with only George for company?"

"It doesn't bother me." She hesitated. "Except that I'd hate to make you or your mother uncomfortable. I know that George will be busy, and many mer don't think naiads are trustworthy, but I'd never—"

"I think no such thing," I said. *At any rate, Pippa has always dealt honestly with us.*

She bowed. "Thank you. Go in peace. Have a good time with Kora."

I arched my neck forward. "And peace be upon you."

I clutched my cloak tightly around my head as I drifted outside. No one turned in my direction, and I was relieved to pass unnoticed through the canals.

As I flipped my fin, propelling myself past the elegant coral homes that populated our neighborhood, I couldn't help but think of the naiad quarter. I hoped Pippa would be able to pay the rent on her house. Maybe she could sell the necklace I'd brought her. If the mob hadn't stolen it.

*The money Mother sent her should be enough to get her by for a little while.* Kora's house lay only two canals away, so I found myself knocking at her door just a minute later.

A male naiad answered the door. "Can I help you?"

"Is Lady Kora in?" I loosened my grip on my cloak so he could see my face clearly.

He bowed. "Come in, Lady Jade."

I floated in after him and sank into a hammock in Kora's ornate entryway. He marched into the depths of the house with rigid, precise steps. While I waited, I admired the black rock walls shot through with bursts of white and gold.

"Jade?" Kora swept into the room with a flick of her amber fin. "It's so good to see you. I've been worried."

We embraced, and she looked at me with wide eyes.

"I really hope I didn't ruin anything between us. I value you and your friendship, and I want to be at your side in all this. It's just—"

"I get it, dear," I said. "You're in a difficult position. It's no one's fault."

"It's Tor's," she said savagely, her jaw tightening. "If that entitled skub hadn't gone and sunk everything off the drop-off like that, none of this would have happened."

"Everything would be simpler," I said, my voice quiet.

"When do you think things will go back to normal?"

I shrugged, hoping the careless gesture hid my fear. *If Benjamin's right that Yvonna wants to overthrow the monarchy, maybe never.* "It'll keep getting dredged up again and again until the trial. After he's convicted or released, maybe a month until people stop caring. Unless his family follows through on their threats and tries to destroy me, which is entirely possible but not likely."

"Yvonna's vindictive."

"But she's also ambitious and practical." It was the mantra I'd been reassuring myself with for days. "If he's found guilty, it's more of a scandal for their family than it is for mine. She'll need to accept the judgment of the king and put this whole thing behind her as soon as possible."

"I hope you're right."

"I have to be."

We drifted to less serious conversation, and I struggled to pay attention while Kora talked about an upcoming party she was hoping to attend. Two or three boys had shown interest in her, she said, and she hoped that after a few more parties she'd figure out if any of them had serious designs on her.

"They're all of higher rank than I am, too," she said with a gleeful grin. "Cyrus is my favorite, I think. He's the sweetest man I've ever met. And his father is the chief historian. He could undoubtedly find me a good apprenticeship to start my career."

"Awww, you're not going to wait until Benjamin's old enough?" I smirked. "He has a terrible crush on you."

"Maybe I will," she said with a glint in her eyes. "He's only four years younger than me, and I'd be Cleo's daughter-in-law. That's even better than the chief historian's."

I gasped in mock astonishment. "Mercenary little siren!"

She stuck her tongue out at me. "You're just hurt that I didn't say I'd be your sister."

"Psh. Prey on men your own age."

"Believe me, I'm trying." She sighed. "Damian's handsome, too, isn't he? But his father's *so* important that I don't think he'd ever look twice at me."

I knew for a fact that at least two eager young mermen of *lower* rank than Kora had fallen all over themselves to impress her, but I supposed she didn't even count them.

*Don't judge,* I reminded myself. *I'll be alright even if I never marry. Unless the anti-monarchists overthrow the king, that is.*

I managed a soft smile, but I longed to be at home in the quiet.

*How odd.* Even though I hated crowds, I spent almost all my spare time with my friends or Kiki. *I've never longed for the quiet like this.*

I managed a few more polite responses, then I floated upward and stretched. "I should go. I'm sorry my stay was so short. Mother will be upset if she gets home and doesn't know where I've gone. She'll think I went back to the naiad quarter or something."

Kora met my eyes, and I knew she was aware that my mother wouldn't be home until evening. But she just said, "Of course. I'd hate to get you in trouble. I really can't believe that you went to see Pippa. If I were your mother, I'd lock you in the house until the trial."

She grinned. I could see the hurt in her eyes, but I didn't have the energy to address the blue whale in the room.

Fighting the sinking feeling of guilt in the pit of my stomach, I pulled my cloak around my face and swam toward the door.

AS I TURNED the corner to leave Kora's canal, I paused. The sound of a merman shouting, his voice deep and lustrous, drew me in. I couldn't make out his words, but from his rhythmic cadence, I suspected he was whipping up a crowd.

*The anti-monarchists?* I'd never been to one of their rallies before, but after what Benjamin had overheard, I found myself curious.

I glided toward the noise, in the opposite direction of my house. After several blocks, I found myself in a part of town that I'd swum through before but didn't frequent. The homes were smaller here and built from duller coral.

As I drew closer, I heard the buzz of a crowd humming beneath the staccato shouts of the speaker. I gripped my cloak tighter around my face. Around one more corner, I caught a glimpse of a tall, bronze-skinned merman with a bright red fin and light blond hair.

"The naiads have been here robbing and raping and killing us for *ten years*," he called. "We're helpless against their water-casting. And the king tells us we just need *patience*. Does the king have your best interests at heart?"

"No!" the crowd roared.

He held out his hands. "Do you think your children are safe while the naiads haunt the city?"

"No!"

I floated in a little closer and found a spot at the back of the crowd from which to observe the rally.

"The nobles are hiring naiads instead of mer so they can afford more servants to wait on their every whim."

"Traitors!" murmured a young merman to my right.

"The king is enriching himself on the backs of hard-working mer and endangering us all with the dark naiad arts!"

A mermaid in front of me bobbed her head.

Whispers of witchcraft and sorcery swirled through the crowd.

"And now our bravest general is on trial over a little naiad harpy?" the leader said, his voice growing quieter.

"No!" called the crowd.

"Not on our watch! Let's tell the king that his experiment is over!"

A cheer rose up from the gathered mer.

"Expel the naiads! Kick them out!" the leader yelled.

The crowd began to chant. "Kick them out! Kick them out! Kick them out! Kick them out!"

My skin chilled. It was time to leave. As I turned around, I ran straight into a mermaid with blood-red hair and a black tattoo of a webbed-foot dragon that coiled from her forehead to her left cheekbone.

"Watch it!" she barked, shoving me backward.

In my scramble to right myself, I lost my death-clutch on my cloak, which fluttered out of my hand and to the reef floor.

Panic pounded white-hot in my veins, and the edges of my vision grew fuzzy as I made eye contact with the tattooed mermaid who had pushed me.

She raised her eyebrows, and a wicked grin curled her lips. "Well, has the little high-class traitor come out to play?"

"Please keep your voice down!" I whispered desperately.

"Looks like we have a little princess here!" she shrieked.

Every eye in the crowd turned toward me. I tensed and turned in the direction of my own canal.

She grabbed my fin and jerked me back. Pain shot up my tail, and I scraped my hands against the sandy seafloor. She yanked me up and pulled me through the crowd, toward the leader who had been railing against the naiads and the king.

I clawed at her arms, but she was stronger than me. When she reached the front of the crowd, she dumped me in front of the merman who had been speaking.

"Andronicus, look what I've brought you!" she sang.

Andronicus's eyes flickered all the way down my body, and I crossed my arms over my chest. I glanced up toward the ocean surface. I knew I couldn't escape the crowd at canal level, but perhaps if I shot up fast enough, I could get enough height over them to slip away.

*If I swim out over the drop-off, they won't follow.* But I wondered if the drop-off would be any safer than the angry crowd if I didn't have Kiki with me.

Andronicus followed my gaze upward. "Don't even think about it," he murmured.

"What do you think you're doing?" I hissed. "You're in stormy waters."

"Vashti, Sula, hold her." He nodded to the red-haired mermaid who had dragged me forward and a brunette mermaid with a violet fin who hovered next to her.

Each of them grabbed one of my arms, and Andronicus drifted up to hover head-and-shoulders above the crowd.

"Lady Jade came to our rally today!" he called. "Even the traitors to our cause know in their heart of hearts that we are right. That the mer will never be able to coexist with these interlopers."

The murmurs of the crowd grew to shouts. I started shaking. *This is getting really bad.*

"Tell me, Lady Jade," he said with a chuckle. "When did you decide to set up Captain Tor for murder? Was it when you took a naiad lover? Or were you just a little pawn in your friends' plans?"

I recoiled.

Vashti slapped me. "The little harpy tried to get away," she said to the crowd.

I tightened my jaw so my chin couldn't quiver. My cheek stung where she'd hit me, but I wouldn't give her the satisfaction of seeing me break down. *Stay strong. Be like Mother.*

Behind me, someone I couldn't see yanked my fin. My gills flared.

Andronicus leered at me. "What do we do with traitors?"

# CHAPTER SEVEN

"What's going on here?" a familiar voice yelled.

The roars of the crowd subsided into a gentle murmur as mer scattered up and down the canal.

I jerked my head up and saw Maximus and a contingent of the Royal Mer Guard. Relief flooded my body. Sula and Vashti released my arms, and by the time Maximus reached me, more than half the crowd had vanished.

Maximus grabbed Andronicus by the front of his burlap wrap. "What the depths are you doing, Ander?" he demanded. "I could have you expelled for this."

Andronicus held up his hands. "For what? I never touched the girl. To tell you the truth, I don't remember who did. There was a scuffle, but I think Lady Jade might have started it."

I wanted to smack the smug smile off his face.

"Do you think for a moment that the king will care about your flimsy excuses?" Maximus said. "You've insulted one of the highest-ranking members of the nobility. If it comes to your word against hers, your word isn't looking very good."

Andronicus smirked. "I have witnesses. Dozens of mer were at the rally. They'll all vouch that the lady wasn't mistreated."

"Listen to yourself. Mother would be ashamed." Maximus shoved Andronicus backward. "Leave, and hope Lady Jade shows mercy."

"Peace be upon you too, *brother*," Andronicus spat. Maximus said nothing as he turned toward me.

"I'm alright," I managed. "They didn't hurt me." I kept my eyes on Andronicus until he disappeared around the nearest corner.

"I can see a handprint on your cheek." Maximus's eyes narrowed.

I gazed at the seafloor and said nothing.

"I'm going to swim with you until you get home," he said. "I don't know that the canals are safe right now."

"Okay." Now that it was over, I felt weak and dizzy. Nausea churned in my stomach.

"Do you need help?" He reached for me.

I swatted his hand away. "No. Thank you, Captain. I am perfectly capable of swimming home."

I started toward my house, choosing one of the smaller, more remote canals to travel down. I didn't want to deal with another crowd of mer. I couldn't.

A minute later, he caught up with me. "You should lay low for a while."

"I don't want to talk about it. But thank you for your assistance. I really am grateful." I forced my gills to move up and down in a steady rhythm.

"It's my job. The king would've had me expelled if I failed to intervene."

"You don't have to brush it off," I said. "No one forced you to accompany me home."

"You're not my favorite mermaid in the city, Lady Jade, but that doesn't mean I want to see you get hurt."

I didn't respond.

"Listen." We turned another corner and entered my neighborhood. "I don't know what you think you saw, but there's no way Tor killed that girl. He's a good man."

"He *admitted* it to me." My jaw tightened.

"I can't believe that." His gaze turned cold. "I'm

sorry you discarded him like you did. But I'm sure you had *reasons*."

Heat rose to my cheeks. "What are you insinuating?"

He shook his head. "I just hope that whatever you're doing is worth destroying a mer's life."

"Why did you rescue me if you think as badly of me as they do?"

"I told you. It's my job, Lady Jade."

I focused my gaze on a clownfish nibbling algae off an anemone. "Well, I'm sorry to inconvenience your day."

I swam ahead of him, ignoring him for the rest of the awkward—but mercifully short—trip home.

PIPPA WAS still at my house when I burst through the door.

"Lady Jade," she said, dropping her mending. "What's the matter?"

"I don't want to talk about it," I whispered, my voice catching in my throat. "Please don't tell Mother I came in like this."

She pursed her lips but didn't press further.

"Is it alright if I join you here?" I asked, struggling to inject a note of brightness into my voice. "I don't want to be a distraction, but I'd rather not be alone right now."

"This is your home," she said. "You have a right to be anywhere you want. And I don't mind the company a bit."

"Do you remember much about the rivers?" I blurted out. "Before the naiads came to Thessalonike?"

She raised an eyebrow. "Of course."

"Were you happier there?"

"I was more innocent there," she said. "And life was easier, at least for a while. Until the rivers started choking us out." Her eyes took on a vacant expression. "I came from the Wye, originally. My people tried to stay when the water levels started dropping. Eventually we moved on from the Wye and its tributaries and tried to find refuge in the Camford, but it was dying, too."

"So you'd rather be back there?" I rubbed my temples.

"Well, of course," she said. "The saltwater chafes our skin. The mer hate us. Most of all, the Wye is my ancient homeland. Imagine if you had to leave Thessalonike and adjust to life in a freshwater river. But my homeland's just not there anymore. A few naiads said they would try to persist in the rivers, but I don't know that they survived. We haven't heard from them in years. Perhaps with a smaller population they found welcome in a healthier river system. But I doubt it. Naiads are territorial."

"Like mer?" I asked with a chuckle.

"Worse," she said. "The Camford naiads almost killed us when we came into their river. Probably would have if their queen Tryphaena hadn't put a stop to it. She's half Wye. Of course, we don't talk about that much anymore. The Wye and the Camford naiads are all in Thessalonike together now. Personally, I think everyone who stayed ended up dead."

"Any of your friends stay?"

"An aunt. She was always more sensitive to saltwater than the rest of us. Couldn't even go on trading trips to the ocean. Why are you so curious all of a sudden?"

I hesitated. "There were some mer at a rally. They want to expel the naiads from Thessalonike."

She shrugged. "Mer have said things like that since we arrived. If the king ever capitulates to their wishes, I suppose we'll travel along the coast and see if the mer of Marbella will take us, at least for a time."

"The idea doesn't scare you?"

"We're still here because it's easier to stay than to go, not because we really think it's the best place for us. Most of us know it's only a matter of time."

"But what if Marbella is just like Thessalonike?"

"Then we'll go beyond Marbella. Maybe even find a healthy river system without many naiads in it. If all else fails, we'll strike out across the deep ocean in search of another coast."

"I doubt you'd find one."

"Maybe not. But if we track an overlander ship, I think our odds are good."

"The king is on your side. As are the nobles, for the most part."

"For now," she said. "For now."

She turned her attention back to her mending, and I took up a blank tablet and a scrib and began to draw.

NATURALLY, Mother had heard all about the incident with the rioters before she got home. I'd known I wouldn't be able to hide it from her. *The perils of having a parent among the king's advisors.*

"Jade?" She swooped in the door, and a sickly sweetness in her voice told me I should flee for the drop-off. "How was your day?"

I dropped my drawing tablet. *Skub.* I glanced at Pippa and then back at Mother.

"I'm sure you have a pretty good idea." I tried to keep my voice even and steady.

"How many times do we have to have this conversation? Do you have any idea what kind of risk you took going to that rally?" she demanded.

"I was the one who got hurt, so *yes*, I realize how badly it could have gone."

She grabbed my shoulders, and I jerked away from her.

Her gaze landed on Pippa. "I'm sorry about Anna. And I'm glad you're okay."

Pippa had gathered up her things into her hands. "Thank you for your condolences, Lady Cleo. I think I should be going."

"No—please stay?" I shot her a pleading look.

Mother said nothing, so Pippa set her things down, gathered the piece of fabric she was mending, and paused to scratch her arm.

"I have an idea," I said. "Crab salad for dinner. Pippa, you really must stay and eat with us."

Mother pursed her lips. She knew what I was playing at, but I didn't think she wanted the fight any more than I did. "Yes. Please do stay."

Pippa cast wary glances between my mother and me but nodded slowly. "I'd like that."

George had left early—Pippa said his father was sick—so Mother and I threw together a kelp-and-cucumber salad topped with crab while Pippa finished her mending. Benjamin arrived home just as we gathered in the dining room to eat.

During dinner, we all laughed until we cried, telling stories about Anna and my father. My heart felt raw by the end, having reveled in the memories and mourned his loss all over again.

"We'll get through it." I grabbed Pippa's hand as sobs wracked her body. "You're not alone anymore."

When she finally left so she could return to the naiad quarter and reach her friend's house before dark, it startled me to realize my genuine sadness to see her leave.

*Somehow, I've become friends with a naiad.* And I was okay with that.

PIPPA WORKED from our living room for the next three days. Halfway through the third day, I set down my drawing tablet and stretched. "Should we go somewhere? I'm tired of being cooped up here. We could take Kiki for a swim."

She glanced at the mending in her hands. "I'd love that. But what if we went back to the naiad quarter today? I think it'd do you good to meet some of the residents. Might help take your mind off all the drama in the city."

A thrill of excitement and nerves ran down my body, all the way to the tip of my fin.

Pippa matched my smile. "Will your mother be upset?"

"Not if we don't tell her," I said with a wink.

"Oh, I don't know if—"

"Please? You suggested it. You said it yourself—it'll do me good."

Her mouth twitched. "If you get in trouble, it was all *your* idea. She'll eventually forgive you. I need to stay in her good graces, or I'll have no work *and* no money."

Her ankle-length, ethereal white dress billowed out behind her as she moved toward the door, and I followed with a flick of my fin.

"Wait," I said as soon as we crossed the threshold. "My cloak."

I darted back in to grab a cobalt cloak—I'd lost my black one for good in the scuffle at the rally. I supposed I should buy another one—this one didn't go as well with my fin and tail, but I still loved it. It used to belong to my father.

"Take that off once we get to the naiad quarter," she said as I tucked my hair underneath it.

"Why?" I glanced at the other mer on the canal. About one in every five wore a cloak, though most hadn't pulled theirs as close to their face as I had.

"Naiads never wear anything that heavy—let alone around our heads—and so few mer come to the naiad quarter, that . . . well, naiads might make wrong assumptions about you—that you've come to buy hallucinogens, or worse—if you're wearing one."

"Oh." I blushed. "Cloaks don't mean anything like that in the rest of the city."

She laughed. "I know, silly. Just giving you a friendly heads-up."

We turned onto the main thoroughfare heading in the direction of the naiad quarter and passed a merchant driving a dolphin-drawn cart full of lovely fabrics that I was sure came from overland trade. I paused for a moment to gaze at the fabrics.

When I turned back to Pippa, she was shaking her head.

"What?" I asked.

"Nothing." She smiled at me. "We just live in different worlds, that's all."

"Well, let's explore yours." I gestured toward our destination.

A few canals later, we arrived in the section of town where the houses grew smaller and duller in color. The wraps of the mer gave way to the flowing robes of water and light worn by the naiads.

I tugged off my cloak and draped it twice over one arm, relieved to swim the canals as myself again.

"Let's go to Camford Canal," Pippa said. "That's where we'll find things to do."

I swam alongside her for two unbelievably slow blocks—she still couldn't quite cast water without pain, so she walked—but when we turned onto Camford Canal, the sights and sounds chased away all of my impatience.

"Whoa!" I pointed to a dancer in the middle of the canal, whose long, blond hair waved out behind her as she spun in a vortex of swirling water.

Her dress, which glimmered in a cascade of cerulean and violet, clung tightly to her waist, but her skirt twirled with the current, flowing around her in elegant waves with each roll of her hips.

She extended her right arm, and the vortex calmed. With a twist of her hands, she formed a ball of water that glowed like the moon and sent it rolling down her arm and over her shoulders.

With a little flick of her other hand, she caught the ball and tossed it into the air. It burst into a shower of glimmering lights that drifted toward the seafloor and dissolved into the current.

I couldn't take my eyes off her.

Pippa chuckled. "Juliana's show is lovely, isn't it?"

"She shouldn't be just a canal performer," I said as Juliana cast an image of a tiny manta ray so lifelike I wanted to pull it into my hand and pet it. "Mer would pay to see this show in the royal theatre."

A broken stone jar with a handful of coins sat on the seafloor about five feet from Juliana. I pulled my purse from beneath my wrap, fished out two large gold coins, and dropped them into her jar.

She smiled at me and cast an image of a dolphin no larger than my hand. It swam toward me and disappeared in a puff of bubbles just as I reached to touch it.

"Come on." Pippa tugged my arm. "There's more to see."

We moved down the canal, and I lost myself in the rhythm of the crowd, which seemed somehow brighter and more comfortable than the gatherings of mer I avoided in the city. I wondered if Father's killers were in the canal with me, but I brushed away the thought.

"I didn't realize there was so much life here." I paused to watch a canal performer play a set of hand drums.

"Well, of course there is." Pippa arched her eyebrows. "Just because things are hard doesn't mean we curl in on ourselves. Back in the Wye, we gathered together every evening to watch the river dancers and listen to music. If we didn't have music and dancing, it'd be like losing the last piece of home."

"The mer have always focused more on drawing and sculpture," I said. "The stories of our ancestors especially."

"Anna said Yvonna has exquisite taste—not that you'd know it from the pretentious art she displays in the main part of the house. But in the back rooms, she apparently has some really lovely pieces." A wistful expression overtook Pippa's face, but it vanished quickly.

"Are you okay?" I asked.

"Yeah." She pressed her hand to her side. "The wound isn't even hurting."

"No, I mean—"

"Yes, Jade," she said firmly. "I'm fine."

Three giggling naiad children burst across our path in a rush of bubbles. When I looked up, grinning at their exuberance, I met the gaze of an amber-eyed merman. His brown hair curled in gentle waves around his shoulders, and his wrap couldn't hide his broad shoulders and strong chest.

*But his face? I know that face.* My heart thundered in my chest. "Alexander? What are you doing here?"

"Oh, you know Xander?" Pippa asked, the creases around her eyes relaxing.

"It's been a long time," I said.

"Jade?" He crossed the canal toward us with a roguish smile. "I'm surprised to see you here. I've heard about—" His eyes darkened. "—well, everything, of course."

"I think everyone has," I murmured, glancing down at the seafloor.

"Oh, not like that. I admire what you did."

I quirked my lips. "Really?"

"Of course. I hope the magistrate convicts."

"You might be the only mer in the city who thinks that," I said with a mirthless laugh. "The king himself is presiding because of how sensitive everything is."

"Wow. That hasn't happened in at least a year."

"Closer to two," I said. "Trial's in four days."

"So soon?"

I glanced at Pippa, who shifted her weight from foot to foot. "At Tor's request. But not soon enough for some of us. I'll be glad when this whole thing is behind me."

He followed my gaze to Pippa. "Hey, let's catch up. Would you ladies eat lunch with me? There's a place down the way that serves an exceptional kelp-and-grouper pod."

"I'd like that." *I think.* I glanced at Pippa, who nodded.

"Sure," she said. "Are you talking about Rowena's restaurant?"

"That's the one."

She turned to me. "He's not overselling the pod. It's the best I've ever had."

I grinned, hoping I wasn't overdoing the enthusiasm. "I can't wait." I turned back to Alexander, and the three of us moved down the canal. "So, Alexander, I haven't seen you in, what, three years? Not since you left school to take that job."

He grimaced. "I'm sorry I disappeared like that."

"Oh?" I said, my voice cool. "I mean, it's not like I really noticed."

"Come, Jade. Don't be like that," he said.

I scowled at him. "You didn't even write."

"I was . . . I was embarrassed I had to leave school. Our friends were all high-class mer like you. I was the only poor kid in our group, and when I had to start working instead, it seemed easier to make a clean break. I know it was immature of me. I really am sorry."

I made eye contact with Pippa and raised my eyebrows. *Not going to get out of the net that easily.* "Well, I'm glad it was so easy for you to forget all of us."

"Are you just coming to lunch with me to pout about how I acted like skub when I was fourteen?"

"You've had three years to find me."

He shrugged. "Didn't think you'd want to hear from me anymore. You're graduated and engaged. Well, you were engaged. Sorry. Bad timing."

A pang of sadness took me aback, but I smirked and stuck my tongue out at him. "You always did have bad timing."

"Depths, Jade," he said, rubbing the back of his neck. "Are you acting all hurt just to get back at me?"

*Of course it hurt, you idiot.* With a cheery smile, I said, "What do you think?"

"I think you were in love with me, and I broke your heart when I left." He winked.

"Oh, naturally, darling," I said, affecting a caricature of a posh accent with a roll of my eyes. "I cried myself to sleep every night."

*You have no idea how right you are.* But I wouldn't admit it, of course.

Pippa smirked at me.

"It was tragic when you got engaged," Alexander said. "But I guess the fiancé isn't around now, so you must fall madly in love with me again." He grabbed my hand.

I pulled away and slapped at his hand. "Don't take liberties. We're not schoolkids anymore."

He drifted backward a moment and studied my face. He relaxed when I grinned.

To be honest, I was still a little mad at him. But it felt good to engage in the banter I'd valued so much back in school. Conversations with Tor had never felt so easy and natural.

*Don't even think about it. Too soon. Far too soon.*

We arrived at the restaurant and gathered around a table in the center of the dining room. I pulled one of the hammocks out from underneath the table and tucked myself into a seated position on it. Pippa did the same to my right, and

Alexander chose the place across from me. After a few minutes, a naiad server came to take our order, and she didn't show any sign of recognition when she turned to ask me what I wanted.

It surprised me. For so long, it had seemed like everyone in the city—or at least everyone on the rich end of the city—knew who I was.

I gloried in the moment of anonymity. It felt like I was back in school, before graduation and adulthood and all the drama of life among the nobility had taken over everything.

"Joking aside," said Alexander, "I really am glad to see you, Jade."

"I'm glad too," I said, surprised to realize that I meant it. "So, what *are* you doing in the naiad quarter?"

"Xander lives here," said Pippa. "And works here, too. He's one of the only mer in the quarter."

"What?" I said, looking quizzically at him. "Couldn't you get a job in the city?"

Pippa shifted in her hammock, but Alexander laughed. "This is still part of the city."

"Well . . . yes, but . . . why here?"

He shrugged. "Why not? I like the people. Rent is reasonable. Don't have to deal with stuck-up nobles taking up half the canal."

He winked at Pippa, who snorted.

I rolled my eyes.

"How's Kiki?" he asked. "You guys still sneaking to the drop-off to swim with the sharks?"

"We hardly ever see sharks, thank you very much."

He *tsked.* "What would your mother say?"

"What *wouldn't* she say?" I muttered.

He chuckled. "What wouldn't she say, indeed."

"Lady Cleo's always been perfectly sweet to me," said Pippa.

Alexander and I looked at each other and burst out laughing.

"Mother's great," I said. "But Alexander and I—and our other friends—tested her patience when we were in school."

Alexander gasped in mock affront. "Speak for yourself. And for Kora, Rhea, and Caleb. They all tested her patience. I just got caught up in the aftermath."

"Oh, so you didn't line our doorstep with sea urchins?"

"Um . . ."

"Or impersonate an inspector to get us—"

"Shhhh," he said with an impish grin. "That one's a secret."

"Ah, yes. You didn't test her patience at all, clearly."

He eyed me. "You were always the ringleader, and you know it."

"Who, me?" My eyes widened.

"It's a wonder you ever grew into a proper lady."

The server brought our food, and I discovered that Pippa and Alexander were right. It was excellent. I liked it more than the stuffy, expensive food the nobles always served at parties or ate on Grand Canal. It was like something Mother and I would make at home when we weren't expecting visitors.

"How's Benjamin?" Alexander asked. "I guess he's probably not a little kid anymore, huh?"

"No." I pouted. "He's the most thoughtful, considerate thirteen-year-old I've ever met. A young man, really. I'm proud of him."

"I don't believe it. I can't imagine him a day older than ten. I'll have to come float with you to see this for myself. And to torment your mother, of course."

I snorted and took another bite of grouper.

When we finished eating, Alexander announced he needed to leave for work. "Can I see you again?" he asked as we drifted out of the restaurant just ahead of Pippa.

My heart fluttered, and I stuffed down the warning blaring in my head. "I'd like that."

"Good," he said, grabbing my hand and squeezing it. "Stay safe, Jade. For real. There's a lot of turmoil boiling in places you can't see."

CHAPTER

# EIGHT

"Well," Pippa said playfully as she walked past me and turned to look me in the eye, "that was fun." She smirked.

"It's not—"

"You guys make a cute couple."

"Oh, no. Alexander's like a brother to—"

"Don't give me that." She crossed her arms and raised an eyebrow. "You were flirting like mad. And I saw the way you looked at each other."

I sighed and looked at my hands. "It doesn't matter. It can't be. The scandal would practically bring down the city."

She rolled her eyes. "No it wouldn't."

"It'd be pretty bad."

"Hasn't stopped you before."

I opened my mouth and then closed it again. She had a point.

"That was a matter of justice." My excuse sounded weak even to me.

A flurry of emotions washed over her face, and I suspected she was thinking of Anna. She pushed it all away with a tight laugh. "Let's go. There are other people I'd like you to meet."

I followed her, noticing shops scattered amid the line of houses, even though this canal was quieter than Camford Canal had been.

The quarter looked so different from the city—*the rest of*

*the city,* I reminded myself—that I struggled to interpret the bustle unfolding before my eyes. In the main part of the city, few canals had both shops and houses on them, or, if they did, the shops sat on the corners where one canal intersected another. Here, I didn't see any way to determine which structures were homes and which were shops.

After a few minutes of floating down the canal and observing which doors naiads went in and out of, I determined that the door curtains hung open in the shops, whereas they remained closed as privacy screens in the homes.

*Well, that makes sense.*

I was attracting attention again, but I guessed it was because they didn't see many mer in this part of town, not because they recognized me as Lady Cleo's daughter.

The naiad quarter was smaller—Thessalonike was home to two thousand naiads and fifteen thousand mer—but it often remained isolated from the rest of the city. Naiads didn't care as much about the distinction between common and noble mer as the rest of us did. All the mer outranked them, anyway.

A number of naiads seemed to recognize Pippa, however, and soon she began introducing me to a steady stream of her friends, all of whom seemed excited to meet me. They'd heard my name, even if they didn't know my face.

*So much for anonymity.*

An elderly naiad with waist-length white hair and a luminous amethyst dress approached us, hands outstretched to Pippa. "Are you alright, my dear?"

"Tryphaena!" Pippa bowed at the waist. "I'm as well as can be expected, thank you."

Tryphaena glanced at me, her eyebrows raised. "I don't believe I've had the pleasure."

"J-Jade. Jade Cleopola." I threaded my fingers together.

"Ah." She locked eyes with Pippa, then returned her focus to me. "I am Tryphaena Camford."

"Tryphaena was queen of the Camford naiads when we lived in the rivers," Pippa said. "Now, of course, we don't recognize any royalty but King Stephanos, but we value Tryphaena's wisdom and leadership."

"It's an honor to meet you." I dipped my head.

"No, Lady Jade." Tryphaena reached out to grab my hand. "The honor is mine. Thank you for your honesty and courage."

"Anyone would have done the same thing."

She chuckled. "No. Most people would have let fear silence them, even if they wanted to report Captain Tor."

My gaze drifted to the seafloor. "Thank you." I didn't know what else to say.

Tryphaena excused herself, and Pippa and I moved down the canal. After mingling for about another hour, we retired to Pippa's house, which was almost repaired. Two of her friends, a brother and sister named William and Miriam, accompanied us.

"The door locks now," Pippa said, "which is the most important part. I'm still not sleeping here overnight because the reinforcement on the door isn't quite done."

"I'll finish that tomorrow," William said. "You'll be able to move back in soon."

"William has done most of the work getting it fixed for me," Pippa said. "I asked the owner of the house to fix it, but he told me I was lying when I said a gang of mer broke in. He threatened to have me imprisoned for damaging his property if I didn't fix it myself. William's been a life saver."

My gills flared. "Who owns your house?"

She shook her head. "I don't want to cause trouble. You can't right every injustice. There are too many in the world for you to take them all on."

I let it go for the moment but determined to check into it once everything settled down. Pushing my simmering anger away, I tried to focus on the conversation with William and

Miriam—something about a petition they were going to take to the inspector who supervised the naiad quarter.

I RETURNED to the naiad quarter twice more in the next few days before Tor's trial began, but I couldn't spend time with Alexander—customers swamped the netting shop each time I went in to visit. He gave me a brief wave from across the crowd but couldn't escape the watchful eye of the shop owner.

With a pang of disappointment, I left with Pippa, and we roamed the canals before retiring to her place for lunch and conversation.

The day before the trial, I found myself at her kitchen table with Miriam and William. A somber mood hovered in the waters.

"It'll be alright." Miriam clutched Pippa's hand.

"It won't bring Anna back," Pippa said, staring at the window.

William folded his hands and looked at Pippa. "I'd give anything to bring her back. She was the best of us all."

"You didn't live with her," Pippa said, a ghost of a smile playing on her lips. "Maybe that's why you always idolized her."

"How old was Anna?" I asked.

"Sixteen," said William. "She would've been seventeen this next storm season."

Something about the expression on his face caught me off guard. I closed my eyes for a moment. "You loved her, didn't you?"

He hesitated, glancing first at me and then at Pippa. "I was going to ask her to marry me on her birthday."

Pippa's hand flew to her mouth, and her chin crumpled. Miriam shot William a scathing look.

"I'm so sorry," he said, standing and rushing to Pippa's side. He placed his hands on her shoulders. "I shouldn't have told you. There wasn't any reason to bring it up."

"No," Pippa said, her voice tight. "I'm glad I know. She always did adore you, you know. Time with you made her happy, and I'm so glad . . ." She choked on a sob.

We sat in silence until Pippa spoke again.

"She was melancholic sometimes, too. She always wanted a meaningful death. Something that would be remembered. That would count for something. That was always more important to her than growing old."

"If the king convicts," said William, "it will send a clear message to the mer that they can't get away with this sort of thing. Anna's death will do a lot to protect the rest of us."

"And if he doesn't convict?" Pippa asked.

I locked eyes with her. "Then we do whatever we must to make sure the nobles—and all the mer—know that this cannot happen again."

WHEN I AWOKE the morning of Tor's trial, I didn't want to pull myself out of my hammock. I pushed away the searing image of Anna's eyes.

*When I testify, I'll have to remember.*

To make matters worse, Pippa would be in the audience. I couldn't imagine talking about what I'd seen in front of her. Or, for that matter, recounting my conversation with Tor.

*Why does it matter?* he'd said. *She's just a naiad.*

And worse: *You of all people shouldn't care.*

Maybe he was right. Maybe I shouldn't care. Maybe my

friendship with Pippa and the hours I'd spent in the naiad quarter were all a terrible mistake.

I floated down the corridor to the living area of the house, where I found Mother eating a breakfast of crab and cucumber.

"That looks good. Is there enough for me?" I wasn't really hungry—the anxiety roiled my stomach too much for that—but it seemed like I *should* eat, if only out of habit.

"Help yourself." She gestured to a second bowl on the other side of the table.

George appeared from the kitchen. "Is there anything else you'd like, Miss Jade?"

"You're here early," I said.

"I wanted to make sure you had everything you need this morning." He crossed the room and pulled me into a hug. "I know this is a hard day."

"Hey, thanks." I tried to muster a smile. "The crab and cucumber looks great."

"I'll put together a snack you can take with you." He turned and swooped back toward the kitchen.

"Try to eat something," Mother said, appraising me with a neutral expression. "You'll want to have all your wits about you when they're asking you questions about what happened that night."

"They're going to eat me alive, aren't they?"

She moved around the table toward me and rested her hand on my shoulder. "Why is it anathema to use a blade in violence, even in self-defense or against a fish, inside the boundaries of the city?"

I stared at her. "What are you—"

"Just answer the question."

"Because it endangers the rest of us," I said. "If sharks or sea dragons were to smell blood, they'd be drawn to the city."

"Exactly. But you're never afraid when you and Kiki find a shark when you swim off the reef."

I looked down at my hands. *So she does know.*

"The shark is the same shark in both cases. But sharks go into frenzy only when they smell blood in the water. If Tor's barrister sees you stumble or look afraid, she'll swoop in for the kill. If you project a bold, unwavering confidence, she'll want to finish the conversation as quickly as possible so you don't have a chance to sway the mind of the king. Try to look like you're comfortable and in control, even though you'll be nervous."

"I don't want to remember," I murmured. "I don't want to go back in my mind and see it all over again. It's bad enough at night when I don't know the images are coming. But to anticipate it all day, to answer probing questions? I've been trying to put it out of my head for a month now."

She paused for a long moment, drumming her fingers on the table. "I won't lie to you. This is going to be a difficult day. A path you might have been spared from had you followed my advice, I might add. But that's neither here nor there. I'm proud of your sense of integrity and the way you held to your conviction, even if I disagree with your method."

I stared down at the table.

She continued, "Your whole life, I've been harder on you, perhaps, than I should've been. It's always been because I wanted to see you succeed in the world as I have. Perhaps I thought it would make it easier for you in the long term. But I want you to know that you've grown into a young woman whom I respect. And I believe the king and the city will see that today."

I risked a glance in her direction. Her piercing green eyes, as strong as steel and as sharp as a blade, fixed on mine. "Uh . . . I . . . thanks."

She floated up from the table and over to the corridor that led to our chambers. "I'll be in the audience watching. No matter what happens, you'll have done a good, just thing today."

I stiffened my spine to stifle the sobs that pulled at my chest.

"Thank you, Mother," I said, carefully controlling my voice. "I'm glad you told me."

WHEN MOTHER and I arrived at the king's court—she'd insisted that Benjamin stay with Aunt Junia rather than attend—we selected hammock chairs near the front of the room, in accordance with Mother's high position among the nobles.

I'd worn a simple but elegant wrap that spoke of my rank but also seemed solemn enough for the occasion. It was made of black cotton—a thin, soft fabric we had to trade with the overlanders to acquire—but remained unadorned and covered my whole torso. Expensive, but subdued.

Mother had tied it in a knot at my shoulder. She'd also woven my long hair into a braid so it wouldn't billow around my face or distract me when I testified.

"There," she'd said, drifting backward to look at me. "You look like the very picture of regal dignity."

Normally I might chafe at such a remark—and certainly at the confinement of a braid—but, under the circumstances, I wasn't going to argue.

But now that mer and naiads had started to trickle into the court, I began feeling self-conscious. *How will I ever speak in front of so many people?*

Tor entered the room, escorted on each side by members of the Royal Mer Guard. I recognized Maximus on his right, and my heart fell.

Tor's barrister, a stocky mermaid of about sixty years, followed him. I didn't recognize her, but I knew she must be one of the best barristers in the city if Felix and Yvonna had contracted her services to defend Tor.

Tor glanced in my direction, a pleading expression on his face, and I turned away to avoid making eye contact with him. Fury and loss warred within my chest.

*Not so long ago, I was so excited at the thought of marrying him.*

I didn't want to think about it, so I focused on the faded pictures carved into the stone walls of the court. Each carving conveyed some event in the history of the people of Thessalonike. The great artists would re-chisel the pictures every few decades to repair the damage saltwater wrought on the artwork. Two panels of wall remained unfilled.

I wondered if they would ever carve something to honor the naiads' arrival in the city. *Or will things always be so strained?*

King Stephanos, wearing his customary indigo wrap that stretched from his shoulders to the base of his ribcage, swept to his ornate gold-and-pearl throne at the front of the court and called the trial to order.

"Loyal citizens of Thessalonike, we have gathered together to render judgment in the case of the accusation of the murder of the naiad Anna Brook against Captain Tor Felicipolos. Will someone make a formal accusation?"

He looked at me, and Mother nudged my arm. My heart pounded as I swam forward several yards and floated in front of the king's throne. I tried to avoid looking at Tor, who sat on a hammock chair on my left side.

The crowd murmured behind me, but I focused my attention on the king. His thick black beard extended almost to his belly button, and a gold crown perched above his bushy eyebrows.

My voice rang out strong and clear. "I, Lady Jade Cleopola, accuse him."

CHAPTER

# NINE

The king nodded. "What is the occasion for your accusation?"

I rubbed the back of my neck. "Thirty-two nights ago, I attended a party held at the home of Captain Tor's parents, Lady Yvonna and Lord Felix."

The king held up his hand, and I stopped speaking.

"Would Lady Yvonna and Lord Felix come forward?" the king asked.

I clenched my hands together. A moment later, I glanced to my left, where Yvonna and Felix hovered, their faces as impassive as stone.

"Did you hold a party in your home thirty-two nights ago?" the king asked.

"Yes," Yvonna said. "But Jade is lying about Tor's involvement in the murder."

The king stared at Yvonna, his bushy eyebrows furrowing. "Did I ask you about Captain Tor's involvement in the murder or about *Lady* Jade's truthfulness?"

Yvonna's voice cracked. "No, Your Highness."

"Then I trust that, at this time, you will restrict your remarks to the questions that are asked of you. You will have your chance to testify freely."

Relief swelled in my chest. *Perhaps the king is on my side.*

Yvonna threw daggers at me with her eyes but remained silent.

"Lady Jade, please continue," said the king. "Describe the events of that night as chronologically as you can."

"I arrived at the party and greeted Lady Yvonna briefly. Then I excused myself to find Tor, who was my fiancé at the time. I—I went out the back door. They have a lovely courtyard, so I hoped to find Tor there. Yvonna herself said I ought to go to the courtyard, in fact."

This time I allowed myself to make eye contact with Tor. The hurt and anger in his eyes tore at my heart.

The king nodded to Yvonna, who said, "It is as she says, Your Highness."

The king's gaze returned to me.

I collected my thoughts and then continued. "When I entered the courtyard, Tor was floating to my right, at the corner of the house. I went toward him and saw him holding Anna's body. I asked—"

"Did there appear to be any wounds on the body?" the king asked.

"Not that I remember, Your Highness."

He nodded.

*That must've been consistent with what the inspectors found,* I thought, relieved. I'd never thought that Tor had used a dagger on her, but I hadn't known for sure. *Imagine the rioting in the canals if he'd used a blade . . .*

"Can you describe the scene in greater detail for us?"

I closed my eyes and clamped my fins. I didn't want to remember.

Mother's words ran through my head: *Sharks go into frenzy only when they sense blood in the water.*

My gills flared as I summoned my courage.

"She was laying face up in his arms, but her head was turned toward me at an unnatural angle. Her eyes were open." I looked at the king. "Captain Tor was perhaps two tail-lengths away from me, so I saw everything quite clearly."

"Pause there, for a moment," he said. "Would Inspector Leo come forward?"

The sallow-faced inspector to whom I'd given my initial report floated forward until he hovered parallel to the throne on my right side.

I glanced sideways. Yvonna and Felix still lingered on my left. I supposed they'd need to give information about the state in which I'd left the party.

"You took the initial police report?" the king asked.

"Yes, Your Majesty."

"And you found the body?"

"I was the highest-ranking inspector at the scene when we investigated and discovered the body, Your Majesty."

"Where was the body found and in what condition?"

"It had been wrapped in fera kelp and dumped in a waste barrel in the naiad quarter."

"Fera kelp, you say?" The king pressed his fingers together.

I wrinkled my nose. *Why didn't he use kena kelp?*

Fera kelp was expensive, usually eaten by the nobility. Kena kelp, which we used to reinforce our homes and weave our hammocks and fishing nets, would've been a much more practical choice.

*Except that he was in a hurry. He knew I might go to the inspectors. He had to dispose of her body quickly.*

The king spoke again. "And how, in your judgment, did Anna die?"

"We found no wounds on the body, Your Majesty, nor any evidence of a blade. It appeared her neck had been broken by a much stronger assailant."

"Thank you, Inspector," the king said. "You may return to your hammock." He turned his attention back to me. "Lady Jade, you may continue with your testimony."

"Captain Tor and I argued after I saw him with Anna's body," I said.

"In this argument, did he confess to the murder?"

"Yes. Well, first he asked me why it mattered whether he had or not."

The crowd murmured, and I waited for it to die down.

"And then he claimed he'd killed her accidentally and pleaded with me not to go to the inspectors. He said she'd been blackmailing him somehow. Threatening to expose his father's business dealings."

"This is an outrage!" shrieked Yvonna. "Can't we all see that this conniving little harpy is in league with the naiads to destroy an entire family of nobles?"

"Madam, you *will* contain yourself," said the king, his jaw tight.

Yvonna shrank back, her eyes on the floor.

"So," the king continued, his eyes returning to me, "you say Captain Tor claimed it had been an accident?"

"Yes, Your Majesty. He said he'd been trying to frighten her, I assume so she'd keep quiet about Lord Felix's business . . . indiscretions?"

"He said that expressly, or you're drawing conclusions?"

I tightened my lips. "I . . . I believe he said it, Your Majesty. At the very least I'm certain that he said he'd been trying to scare her and that she'd been blackmailing him over something to do with Lord Felix's business."

The king nodded. "Take care to be as precise as you can, and state only the facts. You saw nothing to indicate for certain whether the killing was premeditated and intentional or accidental?"

"No, Your Majesty. I didn't."

I answered a few more questions, and the king urged me to recount exactly what Tor and I had said through our whole conversation. I answered as best I could and struggled to look confident even when I wasn't sure I was remembering it perfectly.

My voice shook as I concluded. "Afterward, I left the party in haste. I didn't speak to anyone on my way out."

The king turned to Yvonna. "Did you see Lady Jade leave the party?"

"No, Your Majesty." Yvonna played with the ends of her hair.

Felix nodded his assent.

The king turned toward Tor and the barrister. "Barrister Atlantia, do you have any further questions for Jade?"

I locked eyes with her while she shook her head. "Not at this time, Your Majesty. Captain Tor's testimony will make everything clear."

The king dismissed me alongside Yvonna and Felix, and I glanced up at Tor, who stared at me with a strange expression on his face—his jaw clenched but his eyes relaxed. I couldn't read him, and that struck terror into my heart.

As I turned around to return to my hammock in the first row, I caught Alexander's eye. He'd slipped in the back to watch. He gave me a warm smile that strangely calmed me.

I drifted toward Mother and also saw Pippa, who sat on a hammock several spaces down from us. She stared at the floor, her shoulders shaking with silent sobs.

I sank into my hammock with a sigh. It wasn't over—the king would likely call me forward again to confirm details that other witnesses attested to.

But I'd gotten through the testimony of the initial accusation. I couldn't take it back. I'd committed myself to this course of action. As silly as it seemed—though I hadn't considered backing out—it gave me an undeniable measure of relief.

"Captain Tor, will you answer this accusation?" The king stroked his beard.

Tor's guards released their hold on him, and he drifted forward to float before the king. "I would like to answer Lady Jade's accusation, Your Highness."

"Begin."

"Your Highness, I say this with a heavy heart. As you

know, Lady Jade and I were, until lately, engaged. I loved her. Despite everything that's happened, I still love her."

His voice rang out with conviction, but I detected a glimmer of rage in his eyes when he glanced at me.

"Please describe what happened that night, Captain Tor," the king said, his tone dry.

"The night of poor Anna's demise, I was in the courtyard, as Lady Jade said, hoping she'd come find me when she arrived at the party. My mother's parties are marvelous, but she invites half the nobles, so it can be hard to find a moment alone with someone. Jade and I don't care for parties in the same way that Mother does. Jade and I had contrived that she would come early, and we would steal a few moments in the courtyard together."

My cheeks grew hot. *We had no such understanding.*

"Lady Jade, please come forward again," the king said.

My gills pulsed as I drifted forward, trying to summon the words I would say.

"Did you tell Captain Tor that you would arrive at the party early to rendezvous with him?"

"No, Your Majesty. I arrived early at my friend Lady Rhea Athanasiapola's urging."

The crowd behind me burst into frenzied conversation.

"Is Lady Rhea in the courtroom?"

I twisted around but didn't see her. After a few moments passed with no response, I turned back to face the king.

"We will request her presence to discuss this matter tomorrow," he said. "Lady Jade, you may be seated. Captain Tor, continue your testimony."

Tor shot me another venomous look as I darted away. After a moment, he recovered himself. "I stumbled upon Anna's body perhaps a minute before Lady Jade arrived for our tryst."

*Oh, now it's a tryst, is it?*

"I knew Anna as a servant in my parents' house. She and

I weren't well acquainted, but I had always been kind to her, and we'd developed a friendly rapport. Naturally, when I saw her lying on the seafloor, I rushed to see if I could do anything to save her.

"When I realized that she was beyond help, I picked up her body to carry her inside and send a servant to summon the inspectors. That's when Lady Jade happened upon us. Like many ladies, Jade is of a delicate personality."

My mother harrumphed, and I clenched my fists to avoid rolling my eyes.

"I'm afraid her panic has confused her memory of our conversation," Tor continued.

I swallowed. This wasn't the direction I'd expected him to go with his testimony. I knew what I'd seen, but to someone who still believed in Tor, it would sound so . . . believable.

"In that conversation, I naturally denied any involvement with Anna's death. To my shame, I did ask her if it would matter if I were guilty, since the victim was a naiad. I understand the gravity of that question, and I believe that's what she focused on in her panic. Because of that question, which was a moral failing in its own right, Jade's mind invented a lengthy exchange in which I all but admitted guilt.

"Your Majesty, I will not impugn Jade's character. She believes she is doing the right and just thing. But she is confused, and I hope you can see that. Why would I have murdered Anna in the courtyard if I knew that Jade would come upon us at any moment?

"And Jade?" He turned toward me, his eyes wide. "After all this is over, and my innocence proven, I hope you'll come to realize what a mistake this whole mess was. I still love you. I know you're angry, and I understand why. But at the end of all this, I want to start over. I still want you to be my wife."

White-hot anger flooded my veins. *What a contrived, manipulative speech.* I couldn't even hear the crowd's reaction over the pounding in my ears. *Does he think anyone will fall for it?*

I started to crane my neck to gauge the crowd, but Mother clamped down on my arm with her hand.

"Stay still," she murmured. "Look at the floor."

Pushing down my fury, I did as she said.

The king said, "That is neither here nor there, Captain Tor. Please stick to the facts of your testimony."

Nausea curled in my stomach. I thought I might vomit. Mother grabbed my hand as I struggled to compose myself.

"I'm sorry, Your Majesty." Tor clasped his hands together. "I just wanted to make it clear that Jade is not at fault."

"Did you tell anyone else about your plan to meet Lady Jade in the courtyard?"

"No, Your Majesty."

Tor answered the king's questions for what felt like an eternity. We broke for lunch, and when we returned, the king called for Paulos, a merman who worked in Tor's house, to come forward. As Paulos droned on about Anna's history of employment in the house, my attention began to drift. I let my mind wander, escaping in a vision of swimming off the reef with Kiki.

When Felix replaced Paulos in front of the king, I forced myself back to reality.

"Describe your business, Lord Felix." The king rested his chin on one hand.

"Excuse me, Your Majesty?" Felix asked.

"Your business. Tell me about it."

Felix cast a glance in my direction. "Well, Your Majesty, you know that I trade with the overlanders. Pearls, for the most part."

"I don't suppose," the king asked drily, "that you'd have any idea what Anna could have blackmailed your family with?"

Felix drew himself to his full length. "Naturally, Your

Majesty, I haven't the faintest idea. My records are in order and my taxes up to date. And as you heard yourself from my son—there was no blackmail. Lady Jade's imagination ran wild in that part of her story."

I dug my fingernails into Mother's wrist and willed my mind to drift. *Kiki. The reef. The drop-off.* Rhea had been so frightened by the tiny shark we'd encountered the last time we'd all gone into the deep ocean together, and yet I couldn't shake the feeling that the sharks in the city were far more deadly.

The king finished interviewing first Felix and then Yvonna and announced that we would adjourn, returning the next day for more testimony. With a sob of relief, I fled the court and swam away from the palace and toward my house with all the speed I could muster. My mother followed in my wake.

"Jade!" she called.

I turned around. "What?"

"Slow down. We don't want to get too far ahead of the crowd. Not after all that."

My gills flared. "I can't be here." My voice broke. "I'm about to lose it in front of everyone, Mother."

She rested her hand on my shoulder. "You of all people should know—it's not safe for us in the canals today."

CHAPTER

# TEN

I struggled to hold it together as we kept pace with the dispersing crowd, but by the time we reached home, I had dissolved into sobs that wracked my entire body.

"Depths, child," Mother said, rubbing my back. "We really picked quite the fiancé for you, didn't we? At least you didn't marry him."

"D-did they . . ." I couldn't speak through the sobs.

"Slow down," she said in a calm, soothing voice. "We're all okay. Let me get you a puffer fish tincture."

She guided me to a hammock and moved away toward the kitchen.

"D-d-did they bel-believe him?" I managed to choke out as she rustled through a cabinet.

She sighed, pulled down a clamshell bottle, and swam back to me. "Some of them. Not all." She uncapped the bottle, waved it under my left gill for a moment, and recapped it. "There. That should calm you down."

"Why did he . . ." More sobs cut off my words, but I tried to stifle them to let the tincture—a highly diluted puffer fish extract—wash over my pulsing gills.

"He's giving you—and the king—an opportunity to save face. This way the king can acquit him without suggesting that his advisor's daughter is lying in court. It was remarkably clever, really. Diabolically clever.

"And for the barrister to not even question you in court?

Normally I'd say she was out of her mind, but she's coached Tor very well. She knows it's as important that he wins over the public as it is that he wins over the king."

"It doesn't matter if he escapes punishment if everyone believes him guilty," I said, my voice dull.

"He'd never be able to show his face in proper society again. And for a merman like Tor, that's a fate worse than death or banishment."

My chest heaved. "And his talk of marriage?" My voice squeaked on the word *marriage.*

"He means it, I think. A marriage to you in two or three years sends the message that his acquittal is fully justified. It paves the way for full acceptance into society and lifts the last taint of suspicion from him."

"Skub," I muttered.

Mother chuckled and shook her head. "Obviously there will be no marriage, no matter what tricks Yvonna tries to pull to make it happen."

I rolled my eyes. "The presumption! As if I'd ever."

Mother grabbed a tablet and a scrib and sank into her hammock at the center of the table. "Get some rest. Tomorrow shouldn't be quite as brutal as today was, but it won't be easy, either."

I nodded. "Okay."

*The medicine worked,* I decided. I still felt sad, but the panic clawing at my insides had settled. I flicked my tail to propel my body toward the hall.

When I reached the bottom, I turned back around. "Mother?"

"Yes?" She looked up from her tablet.

"Did I do alright today?"

She gave me a tired smile. "You did very well. I'm proud of you, Jade."

Too many emotions swirled through my head as I drifted up the hall to my room. I sat and stared out the window until I heard the sound of Benjamin's and Aunt Junia's voices below.

Relief flooded me, and I darted down the corridor and into Aunt Junia's arms.

"I'm so sorry, child," she said. "It sounds like it was a terrible day."

I locked eyes with Benjamin and immediately wished I'd stayed in my room or found some way to moderate my reaction. Anger burned hot in his eyes. He spat, "I hope the king banishes the skub from the city forever."

"Watch your language," said Aunt Junia.

He tightened his lips and fell silent.

"It's okay," I mouthed in his direction. Then I said, "Let's be honest—we all hope for that."

Aunt Junia raised her eyes to the ceiling.

"We also have to accept the likelihood that the king will acquit," said Mother.

Nausea overtook me. "You think so?"

"The king needs to save face almost as much as Tor does. Now that Tor's given him an out . . ." She turned to Benjamin and Aunt Junia and explained what had happened during the trial.

My gills flared as she recounted Tor's testimony. When I glanced at Benjamin again, I saw more rage reflected in his eyes than I'd ever seen in him before.

"Let it go, urchin," I whispered to him. "We can't change anything by hating him."

He scoffed. "Can you honestly tell me that you can overlook what he's done?"

I shook my head. "No. I can't overlook it or let it go. I won't ever trust him again. But I'm too tired to hate him anymore."

"I bet Pippa hates him."

"Maybe she does," I said. "She's lost a lot."

"So have you." He chewed his lower lip.

"Let's just get through tomorrow," said Mother. "Today was hard enough without adding anything more to it."

My shoulders drooped. I reached over to give him a hug, then I nodded to Mother and Aunt Junia and retreated back to my chamber. I ducked through the privacy screen just before I lost my composure.

"JADE?" Mother called up the corridor. "You have to get up, or we'll be late."

I lay awake on my hammock, unable to muster the energy or courage to move. Panic collected in my throat at the thought of entering the court. I'd have to see Tor and Yvonna again.

Likely, the king would summon me to answer more clarifying questions or to confirm a sequence of events. That meant I'd have to speak again. In front of all of them.

"Jade?" she called.

I turned my head toward my doorway. "I'll be there in a moment," I said, my voice cracking.

Mother peeked into my room. "Are you alright?"

I shrugged and stared at the wall.

She drew near, grabbed my shoulders, and pulled me into a sitting position. "You can do this," she said, her voice intense but gentle. "You are your father's daughter, and you are capable of anything, just like he was."

"I miss him," I murmured.

"I do, too." She straightened her back. "But we mustn't waste the day in nostalgia. He was a man of action, and he would want us to take action."

I laughed. "You sure you're not talking about yourself?"

"Well," she said, straightening her wrap, "he and I were a lot alike. That's what made our marriage work so well."

"Then where did I come from?" I asked with a soft smile.

She caressed my hair. "You're more like us than you think. You have an unbreakable core. You were the most stubborn child I've ever met, you know."

"Remarkable that you decided to have Benjamin." I stuck my tongue out at her.

"You have no idea," she muttered as she ruffled my hair. "My mother said you were payback for how I'd terrorized her as a child. I expect that someday you'll have to deal with a little girl just as defiant as you were. But you'll be glad she defies you, in spite of your frustrations, because you'll know she has the courage to take on the world if she ever has to. Like you're doing today." She grabbed my hand. "Now get up."

With a deep sigh, I pulled myself out of the hammock, every muscle in my body protesting. "I guess so."

"It's unlikely that the trial will last beyond today. When we come back home, it'll all be over except for the verdict and sentencing."

I clung to that hope as I strung my dolphin pendant around my neck.

TO MY RELIEF, the king only called me forward once that morning to confirm a few minor details about Mother's testimony, and Tor's barrister only asked me a single question.

When Pippa stood in front of the throne, my heart beat faster. I hated that she was being put through the trauma of testifying after all she'd been through.

"Did you notice any unusual behavior in Anna in the days leading up to her death?" the king asked.

Pippa hesitated. "She did seem jumpier than usual, Your Majesty."

"Did she confide in you about it?"

"I never asked, Your Majesty. I just assumed her job was more stressful than normal that week."

"Do you have any knowledge of this blackmail against Lord Felix that Lady Jade spoke about?"

Pippa stared at the floor. "I don't know, Your Majesty. I wish I could tell you more. I don't think Anna wanted to say much without proof. She wouldn't have wanted anyone to—" She choked on a sob. "—get hurt."

The king called for a break halfway through the day, and Mother and I returned home to get something to eat—naturally, George had fixed my favorite salad—and hide from prying eyes until the trial resumed. When we returned to our hammocks near the front of the court, it was Rhea's time to testify.

She looked lovely in a yellow wrap clasped with an emerald brooch at her shoulder.

*It's almost over.* I smiled at Rhea as she moved to float before the king's throne, but she didn't seem to see me. *Odd. I'd have thought she'd be looking for me.*

"Lady Rhea, thank you for coming," the king said. "I wanted to ask you a few questions about the events of thirty-three nights ago, before Lady Jade happened upon Captain Tor cradling Anna's body."

Rhea nodded.

"Did you and Lady Jade arrive at Lady Yvonna's party together?" he asked.

"Yes, Your Majesty." She twisted her hands until they went white. Something in her tone froze my blood.

"When did you arrive?"

"Early. We were the first guests."

"Why did you go to the party so early?"

She remained silent at first. Her voice sounded strangled as she answered, "Jade wanted to get there early. She was meeting Tor in the courtyard for a private lover's tryst."

CHAPTER

# ELEVEN

"What?" I demanded. My gills flared, and pain shot through my stomach like someone had stabbed me in the gut with a dagger.

"Jade," Mother whispered.

The king's piercing blue eyes met mine, and then they returned to focus on Rhea.

I looked to my left and made eye contact with Yvonna, who sat several hammocks down. A triumphant smile curled on her lips.

*What bribe did you use to induce Rhea to lie?* I wondered. I didn't hear anything else until Mother tapped my arm. When I glanced over at her, she pointed to the front, and I realized the king was staring at me.

"Yes, Your Majesty?" My cheeks felt hot. I swam forward until I floated parallel with Rhea.

"How could you?" I whispered.

She didn't reply.

"Lady Jade, Lady Rhea, you have given conflicting testimonies. We must investigate the matter further to decide between them."

*Sharks go into frenzy only when they sense blood in the water. Stay calm. Stay calm.*

"Lady Jade, could you give a detailed account of why you claim Lady Rhea wanted to arrive at the party early?"

A headache pounded in my temples. "She has designs on your youngest son, Prince Theo, Your Highness."

The crowd started murmuring again, but I tried to ignore them. It wasn't my fault that I was being forced to expose Rhea as a social climber.

"She wanted to make sure she was already at the party and talking to a handsome boy when he arrived. She . . ." I trailed off as the memory struck me. "She was going into the courtyard with me, but Lord Philip showed up just before we swam through the door, and she decided to stay and visit with him until Prince Theo arrived."

"Ah." The king nodded. "That's an interesting detail. Is Lord Philip in the court?"

At first, no one spoke, but then a hesitant male voice from the back said, "Aye."

"Please come forward."

Wild hope arose within me, and then I glanced at Rhea and saw terror in her wide eyes.

I looked back up at the king and saw him staring at Rhea. He hadn't missed her discomfort.

*She did this to herself.* It did little to reassure my broken heart.

When Philip reached Rhea and me, the king asked, "Lord Philip, did you happen to notice Lady Jade and Lady Rhea when you arrived at the party that night?"

"Yes, Your Majesty," he said. "I arrived early. They were the only two guests present when I passed through the door."

I glanced over at Rhea. She looked like she might vomit.

"And where were they at the moment you arrived?"

"They were together at the back door. Lady Rhea—" He hesitated, looking at Rhea with an apologetic expression on his face. "—had her hand on the door handle. When she saw me, she said something to Lady Jade and then swam toward me to strike up a conversation."

"Thank you, Philip," the king said, twisting his fingers

in his beard. "Lady Rhea, why was your hand on the door if Lady Jade had set up a private tryst with Captain Tor?" He smirked. "Were you planning on joining them?"

The crowd gave an uneasy chuckle.

Rhea trembled. "I-I wish to recant a piece of my testimony, Your Highness. I'm afraid I misremembered, and I would like to set it to rights."

I looked down at the floor. She could recant in court, but she had irreparably ruptured our friendship.

PIPPA, Aunt Junia, Mother, and I all stared at each other as we sat around the table in the main room of my house.

"We won, I think," I said softly to Pippa.

"We'll find out in five days," Pippa said. "But even if justice is rendered, I don't know if it was worth the cost. What if it doesn't make anyone safer? What if it just angers the mer even more?"

I looked down at my hands. "Perhaps you were right, Mother. Maybe it would've been better for him to be quietly demoted. We could've avoided the whole spectacle."

Mother harrumphed and returned to glowering at the wall.

A knock sounded on the door.

"A mob come to kill us?" I quipped.

"Don't say such things, child," scolded Aunt Junia. She went to answer the door.

Alexander floated on the doorstep. "Is Jade home?"

"Alexander?" I flipped away from the table and darted to greet him. "Please come in."

Aunt Junia moved aside to admit him to the house, and he grabbed my hands.

"Alexander," Mother said. "What a surprise. It's been a long time."

"Not as long as you would have wished, I'm sure," he said with a bow.

She smirked. "You know me too well."

"Alexander and I ran into each other recently," I said, wracking my brain to figure out how much to say without giving away that I'd been lurking in the naiad quarter. "He came to the trial."

"Why don't you stay for dinner?" Aunt Junia asked, forcing a note of brightness into her voice.

"I'd love to," he said slowly, glancing at my mother.

"It's fine," she said, running her fingers through her long, blue hair. "George has gone to the market to bring us back some food. As you might imagine, we're not in any mood to cook."

He turned toward me. "I'm sorry about Rhea. That must've been awful."

"Devastating," I said, my voice flat. "I would've preferred it if she'd stabbed me instead."

Pippa's hand drifted to her side. "Sure about that?"

Mother pursed her lips.

"What?" I asked, shooting her an exasperated look.

"Rhea was scared," she replied.

"What are you talking about?"

"I don't think Yvonna bribed her. She threatened her. Did you notice Rhea's body language when she was testifying? I thought she was going to wring her own hands off."

I crossed my arms. "She was scared because she was about to betray me and worried I'd never forgive her."

"But don't you see?" Mother asked. "That's out of character for her. False testimony against a friend is low, even for empty-headed, social-climbing Rhea. She's always cared about you in her own vapid way."

I shot Alexander a look. *See? She likes all my friends.*

"Besides," Mother continued, "Rhea may be silly and immature, but she doesn't have a vindictive bone in her body. She's too lazy to hold grudges. And if she were only focused on currying favor, she'd side with us, not with Yvonna."

I curled my fingers through my hair. "So, you're saying that Yvonna scared her so badly that she felt like she had to testify against me?"

Mother nodded. "It's the only thing that makes sense to me."

I shrugged. "Unless Yvonna offered her a sizable bribe. But I don't care about her reasons. Nothing can fix what she did today."

"Perhaps not," Mother said. "But I don't think she did it to hurt you."

"Even if Yvonna threatened her or her family, surely there was another way!" I cried. "She could have come to us, and you could have explained everything to the king, and Yvonna wouldn't have been able to touch her."

"I don't think we'll be able to solve it tonight." Aunt Junia placed a firm hand on my shoulder. "Jade needs to relax and think about something else."

I sighed. "I don't know that I can focus on anything else. I just keep going over and over it in my head. The whole trial. What if the king acquits? He can't do so without calling me unstable or a liar or both. We're ruined."

"You're panicking, Jade," Mother said in a steady voice.

Pippa shot me a sympathetic smile. "I thought you were very brave. Thank you. It—it makes me feel like maybe—somehow—the king might convict, even though Tor's so important and Anna was just a servant and a naiad."

"He might not convict," I said. "And you're right—even if he does, it might not fix anything."

"Even if he doesn't, thank you for risking so much."

*If I could do it over, I don't think I'd go the inspectors.*

I muttered, "Don't make me out to be a hero. I don't have the energy for that kind of responsibility."

Everyone remained silent, so I pushed myself up from the table.

"I'm sorry. I just can't . . . I need to be alone. Thank you for coming, Alexander and Pippa. I just . . . I'm sorry." I undulated to the corridor and up into my room before anyone could react.

When Aunt Junia knocked on my doorframe several minutes later, I pretended to be asleep.

LIGHT TRICKLED through my window the next morning, but I lay awake in my hammock for several minutes before I got up. Everything in me yearned to put the whole awful situation behind me, but I felt better after a night of sleep.

At least I wouldn't have to testify again. The smallest kernel of hope bloomed in my chest.

I went down for breakfast and discovered that Aunt Junia was still at our house. "Good morning. Is Benjamin still asleep?"

"He hasn't come down yet, so I imagine so."

"I'm sorry I lost my temper last night."

"It was nothing," she said, shaking her head. "You've handled everything remarkably well, all things considered."

"I don't feel like it." I rubbed the back of my neck.

"I'm afraid I feel partly responsible for this whole situation, you know. Maybe I shouldn't have pushed you so hard to ignore your mother's directive."

"I heard that," Mother huffed from the other room.

For the first time since the trial began, a genuine laugh rippled out of me. "Oh, what a mess we've gotten ourselves into."

Aunt Junia cast me a bewildered look.

"Come," I said, grabbing her hand. "I'm so tired of grief and fear and hiding away. Let's go for a swim through the city and let them see us with our heads held high. We have nothing to be ashamed of."

She raised her eyebrow. "No, we don't, but we shouldn't be foolhardy either."

"Please?" I said. "I just need to feel normal today. Let's go to city center."

She shook her head and sighed. "I'm not sure that a swim in the city will help you, of all mer, feel normal, but I'll go with you if you're determined. Someone's got to keep an eye on you."

"Thank you." I breathed a sigh of relief. I grabbed a tablet and a scrib so that I could sketch one of the statues in the plaza at the center of the city.

"Shouldn't we eat breakfast first?" she asked.

"We don't have to be gone for long. Let's get it out of the way before the canals are too crowded."

"Suit yourself." She pulled a cloak over her shoulders, but I didn't even bring one along.

As we swept out onto the canal, my unbound hair flowed behind me. We turned right and made our way down the center of town. Few mer populated the canals, and for what felt like the first time in ages, I caught only a few stares in my direction.

Kora came around the corner. "Kora!" I called.

She waved at me with a wan smile and swam over. "Jade! I'm so sorry I haven't been around. I heard about what Rhea did—"

"I don't want to talk about Rhea," I said. "How are you?"

"I've been well." She paused, looking at me as if trying to choose the safest topic of conversation. I didn't blame her. "Have you heard about Penelope?"

"Hmm?" I shook my head. "No, what happened?"

Kora leaned in to whisper the sordid details. Apparently Penelope—a recently engaged noble just two years older than Kora and me—had gotten involved in a torrid affair with the married ambassador from Marbella and got caught sneaking out of his house the night before.

*A new target for the gossips.* I almost felt bad for Penelope. That sort of scandal would take serious time to recover from. Perhaps she'd be better off returning to Marbella with the ambassador.

I visited with Kora for another minute until she excused herself, saying that she was to meet her sister and didn't want to be late. Aunt Junia and I continued toward city center. When we reached the plaza, I smiled. Populated by sculptures designed by our most talented artisans from the last century, the plaza always brought me joy.

Everything hadn't entirely returned to normal yet, but we'd surely survived the worst of the maelstrom.

We moved between the sculptures, taking a few moments to study each one. I'd seen them all before, of course, but I never tired of tracing the lines of the statues with my eyes and remembering the stories they memorialized.

There was Eliana—the warrior queen who had defended the city against the invading sirens alongside her brother Nathanael a millennium ago. Her statue, made of blue marble, depicted her wielding a long blade while clutching the dorsal fin of her dolphin.

I moved on to the next, which portrayed Jade, the queen for whom my parents had named me. In it, she extended a basket of fish to a group of huddled overlanders in a dilapidated boat. Her right hand pointed in the direction of the nearest shore. Our legends said that she'd shown mercy to the insurrectionists who'd tried unsuccessfully to revolt against her and that they'd killed her a year later. I reached out and brushed my hand against her face, now worn from the salt and the currents.

My gaze flitted between these ancient women, who had both shown so much bravery. I longed to be like them, but I knew that few had the capacity. If I could barely muster the courage to report a murder, I didn't have much chance of being remembered as they were.

"I want to draw Queen Jade," I said to Aunt Junia, "but let's look at the other statues first."

As we circled around the end of the row to move along the next column of statues, pinpricks like sea-urchin quills tingled down my spine. I glanced behind me and caught the eye of a navy-haired merman.

He didn't do anything except watch me, but his icy stare felt invasive—nothing like the idle gawks I'd grown accustomed to over the last month.

I tried to slow the rhythmic movement of my gills so he wouldn't know I'd noticed him. Looking away, I whispered to Aunt Junia, "Act normally as I tell you this, but I think we'd better get out of here."

She stiffened but continued looking ahead. "Alright. Let's move casually but quickly."

We sped our pace, glancing momentarily at each statue as we swam down the row and back toward the canal that would lead us home. I hazarded a glance behind me, and my heart pounded.

The merman was following us. His silver-and-cerulean fin flashed in the sunlight.

"We're being followed," I whispered to Aunt Junia. I shifted the tablet to my left hand and the scrib to my right.

She pursed her lips. "I told you life wasn't quite back to normal yet."

I chuckled, but it came out strangled.

Someone grabbed my hair from behind, and I cried out as my head jerked backward.

Aunt Junia stopped and darted toward me as the navy-haired mer grasped for my left hand. As his fingers closed around my wrist, I dropped my drawing tablet and, with my right hand, stabbed him in the arm with my scrib.

He grunted, and his grip on me weakened. A thin tendril of blood curled up from his arm.

I scrambled away, launched upward, and yelled for Aunt Junia to follow me.

She kicked forward, and we swam away as fast as we could. When I glanced back, the merman was bent over my drawing tablet like he was trying to read it, one hand clamped over his wound to staunch the bleeding.

"Turn here." We darted down a random side canal. "We'll lose him before we get back home."

"It's not like he can't figure out where you live," Aunt Junia protested, her pace faltering.

"Still, better that he doesn't know we've returned yet." I swept around another corner and down another canal. "Let's sneak in through the back."

"I'm too old for this," she muttered as she caught up with me. Her gills flared.

"Don't let Mother hear you say that. You're two years younger than she is."

She grumbled as we careened down the dark, narrow culvert that ran behind my house. "Your mother—" She gripped her side. "—has always been the healthy one."

I fished the key from my pouch and fumbled with the lock as the frantic energy that had spurred me through the canals dissipated. I prayed that I'd be able to act normally in front of Mother as we slipped in through the back door.

From her hammock, Mother glanced up at us with a raised eyebrow. "Yes?"

I plastered a smile on my face. "We were racing."

"Through the back culvert?" she asked slowly, setting down her writing tablet. Her nose twitched.

"We may have been . . . inspired." I winced. *So much for acting normally.*

She shifted her gaze to Aunt Junia.

"We were attacked," said Aunt Junia. Her gills still flapped at twice their normal speed.

Mother dropped her tablet. "What happened? Are you alright?"

"Jade extricated herself from our assailant's grasp most impressively, and we escaped. We came in through the back so it would take longer for *those elements* to figure out where we'd gone."

I groaned.

"She has the right to know," Aunt Junia said. "And the king needs to hear of it."

Mother rubbed her temples. By the way her left eye twitched, I could tell she was making a conscious effort to remain calm. "Mer or naiad?"

"Mer," I said. "Dark blue hair. Mostly silver tail. I didn't recognize him."

"So not nobility?"

"No," Aunt Junia said. "His wrap suggested he's a laborer."

I hadn't even noticed his wrap, but I thanked the tides for Aunt Junia's steady, observant temperament.

"I . . . may have *accidentally* stabbed him in the arm with my scrib," I said. "There wasn't much blood. I'm sure you'll reassure the king that it happened on accident as I was flailing to get away?"

Mother waved her hand. "It's the least of the king's worries right now, and I'm proud of your quick thinking. There was a riot in the naiad quarter today. The city's going mad. Maybe I should have Benjamin stay home from school this week."

*He's not going to like that.* I cracked a wry smile.

"What are you doing?" I nodded toward her tablet, hoping to distract her from the assault.

"The king has asked me to develop a plan to renegotiate our agreement with the naiads so we can reduce the burden of taxes on the mer."

I raised an eyebrow. "So, he wants to tax the naiads instead?"

"It will be agreeable to everyone," she said. "The naiads' continued presence in the city is dependent on the acceptance of the mer. If we can structure this plan in such a way that the mer know they can't expel the naiads without raising their own taxes, it might help stop the anti-naiad violence."

"And the anti-monarchical rallies," I muttered.

"Naturally, the king is hopeful that we can make inroads against those sentiments as well."

"That's the real reason he wants it done, and you know it."

She didn't say anything.

I shook my head. "I could never be a politician."

"That's a pity," she said. "There's a recent opening on Sophia's staff. I suggested that she offer you the job."

I wrinkled my nose. "Sophia? Really?"

"You graduated school four months ago. With the upcoming wedding, I was going to give you a little leeway, but it's customary to seek out a career by the beginning of the sixth month."

"Well, yes. But . . . Sophia?"

Sophia oversaw the regulation of merchants in the city. If I wanted a political career, working for her would be a phenomenal first job. But I couldn't stand her.

"She's respected and influential."

"She's ridiculous." I made eye contact with Aunt Junia and stuck out my tongue.

"There is that," Mother said.

"She won't go out in public without ropes of overland jewels around her neck, and she always speaks in that absurd, affected accent."

"You know it's a great opportunity, and after everything that's happened, you may not be able to afford to be as picky as you might once have expected," Mother said.

I crossed my arms. "That's not fair."

"That doesn't make it untrue." She was right, and I knew it.

"I'll think about it," I said. "But I really don't think I have the stomach for politics."

"A year working with Sophia would prepare you for a career as either a politician or a merchant. You have a good mind for business."

"I agree," said Aunt Junia.

"Perhaps." I paused. "I'm going to work on my drawing of Kiki. But I promise I'll consider the job."

Despite the morning's excitement, we passed the day in lazy contentment, allowing ourselves the freedom to relax now that the trial was over. The verdict and sentencing would bring troubles of their own, but we couldn't bring ourselves to worry about them.

After Benjamin arrived back home, we ate a simple dinner together. By the time we finished clearing the plates, Mother had started talking about the attack in the canal again. Benjamin cast me a worried look.

"There's a new scandal going around," I said, wiping the last plate clean. "It seems to be distracting people's attention."

Mother scoffed. "Penelope's liaisons? Please. Only the nobles care about that. If—"

Screaming from the canal outside our front door cut her off.

CHAPTER

# TWELVE

"Stay inside. Go up to your rooms." Aunt Junia put her hand on my arm and nodded at Benjamin as Mother darted to the door.

I glanced between Aunt Junia and Mother and then followed Benjamin, but I didn't continue up to my room. He waited for me at the top of the corridor, but I waved him away and hovered above the corridor entrance, just out of sight.

"Skub!" Aunt Junia cried.

I stiffened. Aunt Junia didn't swear. *What the depths is going on?*

Mother's voice rang out over the commotion. "Stop, or I'll have you expelled from the city."

Silence fell over the canal. Coming from my mother, expulsion was no idle threat. She'd had mer banished before.

*But never without undeniable cause.*

Quillpricks ran down my spine. I had to know what was going on.

I swam up toward Benjamin and gestured for him to follow me into my room. We hurried to my window and peered outside.

Darkness had begun to descend on the city, but I could still see Mother and Aunt Junia bent over the body of a male naiad whose face I couldn't make out. A dozen mer were gathered around them.

"Is he dead?" Benjamin whispered.

"I hope not," I said.

"A thousand apologies, Lady Cleo," said a pale, bearded merman who hovered nearby. "But this naiad was skulking through the canal, and I know he works in the naiad quarter. He has no business here."

"Off with you!" Mother yelled.

The bearded mer, whom I assumed to be the naiad's assailant, slinked away.

"Someone call for a physician!" Mother shouted.

Our neighbor, Brendan, nodded and swam away in the direction of the house of physicians.

In a quieter voice, Mother said, "Bring him inside."

Aunt Junia grabbed the naiad's legs, Mother took his upper back, and they carried him toward our door.

Moments later, the door closed, and I bolted out of my room, down the corridor and into the living area. Benjamin didn't follow.

While Mother and Aunt Junia laid the naiad on our table, I strained for a look at his face.

It was Pippa's friend. *William.* My gills pulsed.

Blood drained from a gash that stretched from the middle of his forehead to his temple.

"Will he be alright?" I asked.

"Get some bandages." Mother pressed her hand to the wound.

I hurried up the corridor and grabbed a handful of old cloths and a shell of chilyo paste. Then I rushed back down to the main level and thrust the supplies into Aunt Junia's hands.

"Good instinct, dear," she said, looking at the paste.

She set the bandages on the table next to William and scooped out a thick dollop of paste with her finger.

She motioned for Mother to step aside and brushed the paste onto William's forehead until the wound was covered.

Once she contained the bleeding, she wrapped the bandage tightly around the wound.

"Wake up," she said, grabbing his hands.

"His name's William," I said.

Mother shot me a questioning look, but I ignored her.

"His sister Miriam lives in the naiad quarter," I said. "She needs to know he's hurt."

"The physician will be here soon," said Mother. "We can send word once we have more information to report."

I went to my room to grab my cloak. Benjamin still sat next to my window, tracing the sill with his finger. "How bad is it?"

"There's some blood. He's unconscious but alive."

"Do Mother and Aunt Junia need any help?"

His voice seemed flatter than usual, and I took a moment to study his face. I shook my head. "They've done everything they know to do. The physicians should be able to help more." I reached for my cloak and pulled it over my shoulders and around my face. "Are you okay?"

"Yeah," he said. "I'm fine. It's just . . . this month's been a lot, you know? I don't even know how to respond to any of it, and everything just keeps getting worse. It feels like the whole world's falling apart."

I laid my hand on his shoulder. "We're all just muddling through as best we can, urchin."

"I know," he said with a deep sigh.

"I—I need to go do something. You sure you're fine by yourself up here? Aunt Junia and Mother might be busy for a while, but we could send for George or one of your friends to keep you company."

"No. I'll be fine. I haven't been through nearly as much as you have."

"Doesn't mean it isn't hard," I said.

"I'm almost fourteen. I can handle it." A small smile turned up the corners of his lips.

After a final squeeze of his shoulder, I returned down the corridor.

"I'm going to find Pippa," I said to Mother and Aunt Junia. "She'll be able to tell Miriam."

"You will do no such thing," Mother said in a quiet, steady voice as she checked William's pulse.

"It's the right thing to do. I'm old enough to get married. You can't treat me like I'm a child."

"It is the right thing to do, but you are not the right person to do it. Not now. Not with the unrest in the city. If you get hurt, it will only make everything worse. I'll make sure his sister is notified as soon as I can."

I held her stare for a minute and then glanced down at William. *This is my fault. If tensions weren't so bad, he wouldn't have been attacked. Not in this part of town.*

With a terse nod at Aunt Junia, I swooped out the back door.

---

"PIPPA!" I clutched my cloak around my face with my left hand and knocked on Pippa's door with my right. I hadn't even pulled the cloak down when I crossed the canal into the quarter.

She cracked her door open. "Jade? What are you doing here so late? What's wrong?"

"It's William. He's hurt. Bad. I thought Miriam should know, but I don't know where they live."

Pippa nodded, tightening her lips into a straight line. "Where is he?"

"In my home for now. He was attacked in the canal outside my house."

"Let's go." She stepped off the threshold onto the

doorstep and locked the door. "She lives just down this way."

She extended her left arm, cast a current, and jetted down the canal as fast as I could swim.

A few naiads glanced at me sideways and took a step or two away, but I still didn't pull down my cloak. Mother was right—I shouldn't be seen here, not so soon after the trial.

*Better to be thought a skub in search of contraband or hallucinogens than recognized in a bad part of town at night.*

We turned down one canal and then another until we arrived at a small, rundown house that I couldn't distinguish from the structures on either side of it. Pippa rapped on the door.

We waited in silence until a voice called from the other side, "Who is it?"

"Pippa and Jade," Pippa said.

Miriam opened the door. With one look at our tight, anxious faces, she asked, "What's going on?"

"William's hurt," I said. "You should come."

Her face paled. "What happened?"

"Someone attacked him in the canal near my home. He hit his head and was bleeding when we got him inside. My aunt staunched the wound, but he was still unconscious when I came to find you. They sent for a physician."

She opened her mouth as if to speak, then closed it and ran a trembling hand through her shoulder-length brown hair. Finally, she whispered, "I'll just grab a key and lock up."

When Miriam reemerged, Pippa gave her a hug. "Everything's going to be alright, dear."

"Yes." The tightness in Miriam's voice belied her words. "It will be fine."

I thought of how pale William had looked sprawled out on the table, and uneasiness gripped my chest.

We hastened toward my house. I hoped that William would still be there. *Stay alive. Please, stay alive.*

As we reached the edge of the naiad quarter, I caught a glimpse of a silver-tailed merman on the other side of the canal. My shoulders spasmed as I took in his navy hair and laborer's wrap. A bandage was wrapped around his arm where I'd stabbed him with my scrib earlier that day. Then I locked eyes with him. I tried to tighten my cloak around my face, but it was too late.

He'd recognized me.

# CHAPTER THIRTEEN

"This way," I said to the naiads, pointing back into the naiad quarter.

"What is it?" Pippa asked.

"I'll explain while we move." As we faded into the quarter, I asked Pippa to turn around and glance behind us. "Are we being followed?"

She looked back. "No."

"Let's go up several canals and cross at city center near the statues," I said. "There are more people there. We'll blend in easier."

"Who are you worried about?" Pippa asked as we sped down the canal.

"I don't know. I don't know his name. A merman."

"What does he look like?"

"Navy hair. Aquiline nose. Silver fin with some blue running through it. Broad-chested."

Pippa ground to a halt, her eyes wide.

"What?" I asked. "Who is he?"

"A mercenary. His name's Cassian."

"A mercenary?"

"From Marbella, originally, I think. Came here three years ago and spends a lot of time in the naiad quarter. He's always been nice enough to me, but rumors say he'll take any job for the right price."

"Meaning . . ."

"Some people say he's willing to be a hired blade."

"He's an assassin?" I turned my head to glance back in the direction we'd come and saw Cassian creep around the corner.

"If the stories are true." She cast a look at him and scratched her forearm. "He's never been detained by the inspectors, though. At least not that I know of. It might just be gossip."

"I . . ." I trailed off and thought for a moment. "Let's keep moving."

I pondered the strange, new information, keeping Cassian in my peripheral vision. He still followed several dozen tail-lengths away.

"I don't think he's an assassin," I said finally. "He grabbed my hair. Didn't even pin me to the seafloor. I got away by stabbing him with my scrib. A trained killer wouldn't have been so easy to escape from."

"Unless he wasn't hired to kill you," said Pippa. "Maybe he was just trying to scare you. Or . . ."

"Or what?"

"Take something from you." She bit her lip.

"I wasn't carrying anything valuable. I didn't even have a money pouch on me."

Miriam rubbed the back of her neck. "Well, regardless, if he attacked you, we want to avoid him for now. The *why* of it doesn't really matter. Please. We need to hurry."

I knew she was right, but the discrepancy still bothered me. No matter how I tried to solve it in my head, I couldn't make sense of it.

We careened around the last corner and into city center, barreling past the statues. When I looked down the canal to my left, I saw Cassian drift into city center, his eyes fixed on us. But we didn't have time to slink away and hide.

*Miriam needs to get to William just in case . . . in case the worst happens. If Cassian's determined to catch me, he'll find me sooner or later.*

I quickened my pace, but he didn't give chase. He stopped near the end of the row of statues and watched us. My heart beat rapidly, but I began to calm when I realized he'd stopped pursuing us.

*For now.*

We burst through the back door of my house to find Mother pacing back and forth and Benjamin sitting at the table.

"You're back," Mother said, her voice flat. Her gills flapped at a frenetic pace.

"Where's William?" I asked, anxiety gripping my chest.

"Two physicians came with a cart to take him to the house of healing."

"Is he going to be okay?" squeaked Miriam.

Mother looked her in the eye. "I don't know. His injury was severe, but the physicians seemed hopeful."

Frustration stirred inside me. *For once in her life, can't she say something calming in a crisis?*

"Well, let's go to the house of healing, then." Worry knitted Miriam's brows, but she'd gotten her voice back under control, and it rang out calm and steady.

I admired her. I didn't think I would be as strong in such a situation. I certainly hadn't been when Father was killed.

I said, "I'll come—"

Mother's glare cut me off.

Pippa glanced between us and shook her head. "With Cassian out there, I think we'll be safer without you. And it's not like I don't know how to get to the house of healing."

"Thank you for everything," said Miriam, making eye contact with me. "Really."

"Sure," I said softly. Dull exhaustion invaded every muscle in my body. When the naiads left, I turned to Mother and held up my hands. "I don't want to fight about it. I'm going to go get some sleep."

I WOKE UP late the next morning with an ache in my chest. For a moment, I was disoriented, and then I remembered. *William.*

I pulled myself out of my hammock and meandered down the corridor to see if Mother was still home. To my relief, she had already left, probably for the palace. We'd be able to delay the fight.

It was George's day off, and I didn't want to be alone all day while Benjamin was at school. I grabbed a quick breakfast, put on my plainest wrap—Rhea would never allow herself to be seen in such a garment—and set off for the house of healing, hoping against all hope that William had pulled through the night.

Though I remained on my guard, I reached the house of healing without seeing any sign of the mysterious Cassian. When I entered, I asked the young mer at the front if she had any news on the naiad who'd been brought in the night before.

"You a friend of his?" She scanned me. "Weren't you in with that other naiad a few days ago?"

"Yes, and yes."

She shrugged. "Not any of my business, I guess. He was alive last I heard. Last room on the left. Go on back. His sister's still here."

I nodded, relieved that she hadn't connected my face to Tor's trial. Then again, my wrap didn't exactly scream *noble.* I moved into the corridor and drifted toward the room she'd indicated.

I floated into a room where Miriam sat on the edge of a bed. "Hey."

"Hey," Miriam said, her eyes swollen and heavy.

"How is he?"

"Holding on. The physicians said if he made it through the night, his chances were good, so I'm optimistic."

"Oh, good," I said with a sigh of relief. "You doing okay?"

"I'm fine," she replied. "Or I will be, anyway. It's a shock, you know."

"I understand," I said. "I really do. I—I lost my father quite suddenly to violence a few years ago."

"I'm sorry. I remember when that happened. Some naiad kids killed him, didn't they?"

"That's what everyone thinks. The inspectors called it an accident, but that was just to smooth things over. Naiad liberationists, the rumors say."

Miriam shook her head. "I can't imagine."

"We just had to learn to live with it. Father wasn't a vindictive person, which helped. It wouldn't have mattered as much to him whether they found the killer or not."

"Did you see who did this to William?"

I thought for a moment, rubbing the back of my neck. "I think so. I don't know for sure. But Mother did. I'm sure she filed a report with the inspectors."

*Am I sure? She didn't want me to report Tor.* I pushed the thought to the back of my head.

Miriam nodded, her soft brown eyes meeting mine. "Thanks for checking in on us."

"Is Pippa at home?"

"As far as I know. She left an hour or two ago, when we knew he'd made it through the night. I'm sure she's resting now."

"You should rest as well."

Miriam shook her head. "I need to be here in case anything changes."

I thought about inviting her to sleep at my house. After all, Mother and I lived much closer to the house of healing than she did—but something stopped me.

I was already seen as a naiad-lover. It wouldn't do to have

them traipsing in and out at all hours of day and night. The neighbors would talk, and mer would tease Benjamin at school. It was bad enough that Pippa was around all the time, but at least we could say she worked for us.

"Alright. I'm glad that . . ." I hesitated. "I'm glad it looks like he's coming through."

As quickly as I could, I turned around and hurried out of the room and down the hall. Heat flushed my cheeks. I hadn't known what to say, and the awkwardness embarrassed me. I needed to get home.

*And hope that I get there before Mother returns and finds me gone.*

FOR ONCE, luck proved to be on my side. The house was quiet when I returned. I carefully locked the door behind me and decided to pick up the drawing I'd started of Kiki weeks ago. I had just finished the shading on her fins when I heard a *thunk* come from the level above me.

I froze. *That's odd. Is Mother home after all?*

I set down my scrib and listened more closely. I thought I heard a slight swish, like a fin flicking through the water. I darted into the kitchen and looked for anything I could use to protect myself.

I grabbed a knife with shaking hands. *Just in case. Better exiled than dead.*

I stared at the entrance to the corridor, the knife in my hand. Several more heartbeats passed with no sign of danger.

I felt silly. But then I shook my head. I might have imagined the fin, but I hadn't imagined the sound of something falling. I shifted the knife from hand to hand, wondering if I should stay there, armed, or flee the house.

*Surely it's nothing. It's Mother or Pippa or Benjamin.* But I was too petrified to call out.

The silence lingered another minute.

Then Cassian burst out of the corridor and into the room.

Time stretched out, and I saw each detail in precise, unforgiving clarity as he jolted toward me. His tight jaw. The tension lines around his eyes. A smooth scar running from his ribs down to his scales. If he carried a blade of his own, it was well concealed.

I didn't have the presence of mind to scream. When he grabbed my wrists, the knife in my hand sank to the floor.

He shoved me against the wall. "Where is it?"

# CHAPTER FOURTEEN

"Where is what?" I flailed, struggling against his grip.

He rolled his bright blue eyes. "Playing dumb isn't cute, *milady*. I need the tablet that Pippa hid here. I don't like killing bystanders, and it'll be a skub of a mess if I have to kill you. Just give it to me, and you'll never see me again."

"What . . . tablet? What the *depths* are you talking about?"

He tightened his grip on my wrists. "The naiads told you who I am, yes?"

"They passed on the rumors they'd heard," I said with a growl, trying to extricate one of my wrists from his grasp.

"Then you know I'm not to be trifled with."

Fear stabbed my heart. "I—I can't give you what I don't have. Please. I don't have any idea what you're talking about."

"My employer wants to use it to bring Felix to justice," he said. "You'll lose a little leverage once it's public, but that's offset by the damage it will do to Felix's reputation. He and Yvonna won't be able to touch you. They'll be ruined."

"Depths! I don't know what you're talking about! I'd give it to you if I could."

"My employer will pay you for it. Or you can keep hiding it and die."

Exasperation drove out my fear. "If you're so convinced I'm hiding it, why kill me? How do you plan to find it if I'm dead?"

He stared into my eyes, and I tilted my chin upward in defiance. Finally, he broke the stalemate. "You really *don't* know. But it must be here. Pippa fled with it from her home the day the vandals tore through. She came here with you."

"Pippa's in and out of here often. She probably took it back some other time."

He shook his head. "She's been watched, carefully. It's here."

"Then find it!" I spat. "And get out of my house."

He released my hands. "Has Pippa been here unsupervised?"

"I thought you guys had been watching her carefully."

He shot me a warning look.

Realization dawned on me. "Yesterday at the statues. You thought I was carrying it. That's why you didn't pursue us."

He grunted.

"But it was just a blank tablet for drawing."

"Would've been better for you if you'd had it with you," he said.

"Look for it," I said. "I won't stop you. Tear the house apart if you have to. But Mother will be home soon, and given her connections, I don't think you want to explain this to her, so move fast."

He gestured for me to swim in front of him. "Stay in front of me, where I can see you. I've just about finished."

I held up my hands and complied. I couldn't have explained why, but his presence just didn't fill me with the terror that the situation probably justified. Which was odd for me. *But I really don't think he wants to kill me.*

I crossed my arms when he guided me into my room and continued his frantic search.

The door opened and closed a level below us, and Cassian held up one finger over his mouth.

"Jade?" Mother called.

"Hi, Mother," I said, looking at Cassian.

His face tightened. He threw open one more drawer and rifled through it. The tablet wasn't there.

Glaring at me, he opened my window and darted away on the current.

THREE DAYS passed without any sign of Cassian. I knew I should tell Mother about his threats, but I just couldn't. She'd freak out again, and I couldn't handle more tension and drama. Neither could Benjamin—he faced enough of it at school.

The morning of the third day, I awoke with a sick feeling in the pit of my stomach. *Today they announce the verdict.*

I wanted to believe that they'd convict my skub ex-fiancé, but at the end of the day, Tor was right. I now knew Anna as Pippa's sister and William's sweetheart. But to the king?

*She's just a naiad.*

It was naive to think that the king would risk convicting Tor for the murder, even if he wanted to. But I would attend the sentencing and hold my head high, like the ancient queens Eliana and Jade. I might not ever possess their strength and dignity, but at least I could prove myself a worthy citizen of their kingdom.

I floated over to my closet to find a wrap for the sentencing. As I inspected my garments, I saw a glimpse of gray at the back and pulled it out. I smiled.

"You don't belong back there, silly," I murmured.

It was a simple but regal stone-gray wrap, as soft as a fuzzfish. One of my favorites. I hadn't gotten a chance to wear it in weeks because it'd had a tear in it. I pulled it off the pole and began to wrap it around my torso, but then I stopped.

Something wasn't right. A section of the wrap felt stiff like . . . *Like there's something sewn inside.*

I ran my hand across it. Whatever was hidden in the wrap was hard, thin, and rectangular, about two hand-lengths tall and one across.

*Like a tablet.*

A thrill ran down my body. So this was what Cassian had been looking for. Pippa must've sewn it into the wrap to hide it and pushed it into the back of my closet so I wouldn't discover it.

I dropped the wrap on the floor, tucked my sleeping wrap back around my body, and darted down the corridor to grab a knife.

"Morning, Jade," said Aunt Junia.

I pulled up short. "You're here early."

"I'm coming to the sentencing with you," she said. "Moral support, you know."

I smiled at her. "Thanks, Aunt Junia. You've been a rock through all this."

"Breakfast?" she asked.

"Not yet," I said. "There's a—a thread loose on the wrap I'm planning to wear. I need to grab a knife to trim it off."

"Mmm-hmm," she said. "Be careful not to tear it."

"I will."

I hurried back up the corridor and laid the wrap on the windowsill. I hesitated when I positioned the knife along the seam. Did I really want to know the information Cassian seemed so desperate to get his hands on?

For that matter, did I really want to destroy one of my favorite wraps?

*Yes. Yes I do.* Pippa would be able to fix it. With shaking hands, I ripped seam by seam along the area parallel to the tablet until I had a hole big enough to pull it out. I scanned it and then furrowed my brow.

*This* was what Cassian had attacked me in broad

daylight for? In my hands I held a list that looked like a trade invoice.

It showed the amount that Tor's father had been paid by an overlander named John Taylor for a single white pearl. Nothing about it looked peculiar. Overlanders paid extravagant sums for pearls, and I knew that Tor's father dealt in them.

*But it can't just be a pearl. That's not something he'd need to hide.*

A chill took hold of me as I wondered if Tor had been telling the truth about the blackmail. Maybe this, somehow, was the information Anna had been killed over. It would explain Cassian's ravings.

I pushed the thought away. I'd have time enough to dwell on it later.

I studied the tablet for a few minutes to no avail, then decided I'd ask Pippa about it after the sentencing. I stuffed the torn wrap and the tablet into one of the drawers I'd seen Cassian search already, returned to my closet, and selected a light blue wrap dotted with pearls.

*Absurd that the overlanders pay so much for them, if you ask me.* I finished wrapping it around myself and secured it with a small conch clasp, then I picked up my dolphin pendant and hung it around my neck.

"There," I murmured, looking in the mirror. Satisfied, I drifted down the corridor to leave for the sentencing with Aunt Junia and Mother.

"You look lovely," Aunt Junia said when I returned. "You're sure you don't want breakfast?"

Nauseated, I shook my head. "I can't eat. Not until after."

Mother furrowed her eyebrows. "I think you should eat something."

"I can't," I said firmly.

"If you say so." Aunt Junia shrugged.

Benjamin emerged from the corridor, dressed in a school-uniform wrap.

"Hey." I floated over to hug him. "Are you sure you want to go to school today? No one will fault you if you stay home. I'll talk to Principal Lira myself."

He shook his head. "Mother didn't want me to go today either, but I talked her into it. If I don't go, it's sort of like Tor wins a little bit, you know?"

I smiled. "I know. I'm proud of you. You know that?"

He grinned at me. "I'm proud of you, too."

I rolled my eyes and ruffled his hair. "Eat your breakfast, and get out of my sight."

He stuck his tongue out at me and turned toward the table. "I'll eat Jade's breakfast, too."

"You overhear entirely too much," said Mother. "But yes, there's plenty of food."

I swam back and forth across the room until Benjamin left for school. As soon as he closed the door behind him, I said, "Let's just go now. I know we'll be early, but I can't handle waiting here."

Mother nodded. "I think we'll all feel better when we get there."

I doubted that, but I wasn't going to protest. I needed to escape the house.

*Maybe I'll go find Kiki, and we'll swim off somewhere together and never come back. I bet there are cities of mer so far away that no one from Thessalonike would ever track us down.*

It was an absurd thought, but I took comfort in it during our swim to the court, past the long line of houses belonging to the nobles.

It struck me how different everything looked from the naiad quarter. Almost ostentatious by comparison. I wasn't sure I liked it all that much anymore.

A young naiad girl—perhaps ten—lugged a large, covered bucket out of one of the houses. I wondered what was in it and why she was working at such a young age.

*Then again, why did Alexander have to quit school to work?*

A deep, heavy sigh racked my body.

"What's the matter, dear?" Aunt Junia asked.

"The city's just such an unfair place," I replied.

Aunt Junia chuckled. "Yes, it is. So's the rest of the world."

"You've never left the city. How would you know?"

"We all know the stories," she said. "Besides, why wouldn't it be? Why would you expect one city to corner the market on good or evil?"

"I suppose so," I said. "Even Tor isn't all bad."

She huffed.

I tried to suppress a smirk. "I'm serious, though. I mean, sure, he's entitled and manipulative and, well, a murderer, but . . ."

*But he's loyal to a fault.* I couldn't get the tablet out of my head.

"But what?"

I shook my head. "Nothing. I guess I've just been wondering if he told me a half-truth that night. Maybe he *was* trying to protect Felix from some kind of embarrassing revelation."

She pursed her lips at me.

"What? It's not like it excuses murder or anything. But maybe he felt trapped between two bad options and just made the wrong choice in that moment."

"Well, he may not be all bad, but he's certainly bad enough," Aunt Junia said with a *hmmph*.

I fell silent as we turned the corner and passed under the solid marble archway that marked the entry to the king's palace. I hesitated.

"Court's this way." Mother jerked her head to the right.

*Of course I know where the court is,* I wanted to retort. But I kept silent.

Instead, I closed my eyes and imagined myself swimming off the reef with Kiki. When I opened my eyes, I couldn't stop the dread from clenching in my chest.

"Are you ready?" Aunt Junia asked, her forehead creasing.

"Should I be?" I tried to force a smile.

"You don't have to be," she said. "You just have to get through it, and we'll be here to help you no matter what."

I turned to Mother, emotion brimming in my throat. "I'm sorry I dragged you through all this. I know it hasn't made your life easier."

She met my gaze. "Like I told you during the trial, Jade, I'm proud of you for following your moral current even though the tides were against you. If your father were here, he'd be proud, too."

We entered the court, and my stomach felt as heavy as a boulder. I'd expected that we'd be the first to arrive, but we weren't; Yvonna already sat in a hammock at the front, her fin curled up underneath her and her arms crossed over her chest.

When we passed by her, she sat up quickly and pasted a stiff smile onto her face.

"Lovely to see you," she said in a sharp, biting tone. "I'm so looking forward to my son's vindication today and the end of your schemes." She brightened. "Perhaps the king will even make you go to trial for filing a false report and trying to destroy a merman's life."

My lips tightened into a thin line. "Your son killed someone, Yvonna. I don't know if you refuse to believe it or if you're intentionally covering for him, but the king can see through *all* of you."

She scoffed and studied her fingernails. "I will not dignify your impudence with a reply."

*You just did.* I shrugged it off.

"That's enough, Jade." Mother grabbed my elbow. "Let's take a seat before anyone else gets here."

I wanted to rage at Yvonna, to tell her that she and the rest of her disgraceful family could sink to the depths for all I cared, but one look at Mother's stern face dissuaded me.

*No need to cause yet another incident.* I'd instigated enough drama to last a lifetime.

I sank into a hammock chair in the front row, several spaces away from Yvonna, and tried to shut out everything around me as mer and naiads filtered into the room.

Just before the appointed start time, Pippa walked in, her lips tight and her eyes heavy, and took a seat behind me.

I turned to ask her about the tablet, but she leaned forward and whispered, "William took a turn for the worse. We don't know if he'll make it through the day."

My heart dropped. "Depths. How's Miriam?"

Pippa's chin quivered. "She's a wreck. We all are."

"Are you sure you want to be here?" I asked, grabbing her hands.

"I have to be. Anna would want me to see this through."

I sucked water through my gills. "Pippa, I know this isn't a good time to ask you this, but I found—"

"His Majesty, King Stephanos of Thessalonike!" yelled a herald from the front of the room. A hush fell over the crowd, and I turned back to the front.

The king swept in and took his seat on the throne. "I hereby call this hearing to order."

I hazarded a glance at the room, looking for Alexander, but I couldn't find him in the crowd. Every hammock in the room had been taken.

Instead, my gaze settled on Felix. I narrowed my eyes in thought. Then I tore my focus away, no closer to an answer. Tor floated several tail-lengths in front of the throne.

Yvonna and I looked at each other, and something like fear shone in her eyes, stronger even than her venom.

My gills pulsed, and my heart pounded. *This is it.*

CHAPTER

# FIFTEEN

"We are here today," said the king, "to render the verdict against Captain Tor Felicipolos of the Royal Mer Guard on the accusation of the killing of the naiad Anna Brook."

*Please say guilty. Please say guilty.*

The king drummed his fingers on the side of his throne. "On that charge, Captain Tor's transgression is apparent. He is declared guilty."

The room burst into a cacophony of noise as mer rose in protest and naiads cheered.

Relief washed over me. I thought the sobs that I'd worked so hard to restrain might burst forth from my chest at any moment. Tor held perfectly still, and I wished I could see his face.

"Silence!" called the king, his face stern and his beard wagging. "We are not yet finished."

The members of the Guard who floated on either side of the king tightened their fingers on the clubs strapped to their fins, and the room quieted.

"Yet," said the king, "there is insufficient evidence that Captain Tor planned the killing in advance or even that he intended to commit it when he initiated the attack. As a result, his sentence is mitigated."

The mood of the room lightened, and my exhilaration gave way to confusion.

"Captain Tor," he continued, "you are hereby stripped of your military rank and expelled from the Royal Mer Guard. You will remain under house arrest in your parents' home for a period of one year, during which time I expect you to reflect on the severity of your actions and their consequences. Should you commit such an egregious offense again, I will have no choice but to banish you from the borders of the city or commend you to the currents of the fountains of the deep."

The crowd's murmuring grew louder. I looked behind me and made eye contact with Pippa, who had tightened her hands into fists. Yvonna trained baleful eyes on me.

"Well," muttered Aunt Junia, raising an eyebrow. "That's a verdict to anger everybody, isn't it?"

"*Silence,*" hissed the king in a low, dangerous tone.

The crowd quieted again, but I sensed a swell of emotion lingering just beneath the surface, like the aftereffects of a lightning strike. The water nearly crackled with it.

"I expect every citizen of Thessalonike, mer and naiad alike, to abide by the verdict I have decreed," he said. "The Royal Mer Guard will escort Sir Tor back to his home to begin his sentence. You are dismissed."

I rose from my hammock. So many emotions collided in my chest that I despaired of sorting them all out. But at the bottom of them all, a refrain resounded in my head: *We won. We won. We won.*

I turned back to Pippa. She sat still, her face pale, her hands clenched in her lap.

"Come on." I reached for her shoulder. "Let's get out of here to give things a chance to settle down. Everyone looks tense. It could get dangerous."

She batted my hand away but remained still otherwise.

"Pippa?"

"Leave me alone," she whispered. "Please."

"It's okay, Jade," said Aunt Junia. "She's had a shock. Several, in fact. She needs time."

"I have to ask her about something," I said. "It's important."

"Not right now. Let's go." Aunt Junia grabbed my elbow. "We're going home."

I didn't look at Tor on my way out.

UNREST SIMMERED in the city. Each day when George reported for work, he shook his head. "The canals are uneasy," he said. "I wouldn't go out if I were you, Miss Jade."

Stir-crazy though I was, I decided not to tempt the tides. Instead, I stared out my window, watching the traffic on the canal and pondering the strange tablet. Benjamin came in periodically to try to cheer me up.

"Hey, Jade," he said. "I just tore a hole in my hammock with a dolphin tooth."

I furrowed my brow and stared at him. "What are you talking—"

"But I don't think Mother will be mad," he said, grinning, "because I didn't do it on porpoise."

I groaned, but a wisp of a smile turned up the edges of my lips.

Mother yelled from down the hall, "Not even your father would have thought that was funny."

He socked my arm. "What do you think?"

Arching an eyebrow, I said, "Well, you should probably stay in school rather than trying to make it as a teenage comedian."

"When I'm famous, you'll wish you'd been more supportive," he said, blocking my face with his hand.

"Suuuuure," I said, reaching out and poking him in the side.

He squeaked, and the tips of his ears turned bright red.

"Well, *that* made me feel better," I said with a devilish grin.

"Benjamin, have you done your schoolwork yet?" Mother called.

"You don't get my genius," he shouted with a dramatic swish of his hair. Then he sauntered out of my room.

I suppressed a chuckle and resumed my silent vigil at the window with a lighter heart and a little more hope.

On the fourth morning after Tor's trial, while Mother sat at the table finishing breakfast, I swam back and forth across the bottom level of the house. *This is intolerable.* I was maddened enough to seriously consider working for Sophia the Ridiculous if it would release me from the monotony of what felt like my own house arrest.

George entered the house with his face furrowed into deep lines.

"What is it?" I asked, my jaw tightening.

"The naiads are rioting," he said. "All through the quarter."

Mother's eyes widened. "What happened? Was it the sentencing?"

George rubbed his temples. "That's part of it, I'm sure. Another naiad girl's gone missing, and a gang of mer destroyed several homes last night, they say."

Nausea threatened to overwhelm me. *Don't riot,* I wanted to scream. *Don't you know it'll only make things worse?*

But would it really? Could things really get worse?

*Of course they can.*

Mother's eyes widened. "How bad are the riots?" she asked, reaching for her cloak. "I've got to get to the palace."

"Bad enough," he said. "Word on the canal was that the Royal Mer Guard was losing control over the quarter. It's probably an exaggeration—you know how people talk—but . . ."

She closed her eyes for a moment. "Foolish, foolish," she muttered. She kissed the top of my head and darted out the door.

I thought of Alexander and wondered if he was alright. It couldn't be safe for a mer who lived in the quarter, even if the naiads knew him.

The liberationists had lain low for years—ever since they'd killed Father—but they were still walking free, and I suspected they'd incited the rioting.

"Pippa found me in the canal on my way here," George continued. "She wanted me to tell you that William is awake and talking."

I stared at him. "After so long? I thought for sure we'd lost him."

"I'm pleased to say that we have not. At least not yet."

"Thanks for telling me, George," I said. "I—I'm going to go up and get a bit more rest."

"Are you sleeping well?" His eyes narrowed in concern.

I smiled softly at him. "Not very well, no. But I'll be fine. It's just a lot to process—so much, in such a short period of time."

I didn't tell him that nightmares about Tor and William and Anna had awakened me every night since the sentencing. Sometimes more than once.

"I'll bring you some bubbleweed paste tomorrow. Put it on some kelp and eat it after dinner, and it'll help you sleep," he said.

"Thanks, George," I said. "I don't deserve someone as loyal and dependable as you."

He smiled at me and ruffled my hair. "I've worked for your parents since before you were born, Miss Jade. I watched you grow up. You deserve a lot better than what you've gotten these last weeks."

I closed my eyes. "Thank you, George. You mean the world to us."

"Go get your rest," he said. "You need it in these trying days."

"Kora's still keeping her distance," I blurted out. "And, of course, I never want to see Rhea again. Pippa hasn't spoken to me since the verdict was announced. And Mother is gone all the time trying to help the king maintain order in a city gone mad." I felt sobs building in my chest. "I can't take this, George. I just can't."

My face crumpled, and I wrapped my arms around my body.

He pulled me into a hug. "Oh, Miss Jade. It'll be alright soon."

I sniffled. "How do you know?"

"Well, it can't get much worse, can it? That means it's got to get better."

Part of me wanted to point out the flaws in his logic, but the rest of me just wanted to rest in his comforting, fatherly hug.

"Thanks," I murmured.

"Now then," he said, releasing me and clearing his throat. "Take your nap, and when you wake up, I'll have sweet puffs for you to eat."

I couldn't imagine I'd be hungry, but I nodded and tried to look enthusiastic.

He chuckled and patted my back. "You've never been able to fool me. But I think you might be more interested in them when you wake up."

I drifted up to my room, exhaustion weighing me down. I felt like I had to push myself through the water just to get up the corridor. I hoped I'd dream of George's sweet puffs.

Instead, I dreamed about Anna.

"MISS JADE?" George called up the corridor. "You have a visitor."

I lay in my hammock, still not craving sweet puffs. Sorrow weighed on every muscle in my body, but curiosity and an ever-present sense of duty pushed me out of my hammock.

I glanced at my reflection in the mirror. My hair was a bit tangled, and I certainly didn't look rested, but my wrap was still proper.

I shrugged. It wasn't like my hair mattered. I doubted my guest could be anyone important.

I glanced down at the drawer in which I'd tucked the tablet, in the middle of a stack of clean tablets for drawing. If Cassian came back looking for it, there wasn't much I could do to stop him. But I'd seen him look through that drawer already . . .

I floated down to the main level of the house and stopped short. "Alexander? I'm surprised to see you here."

Now I wished I'd taken the time to run a comb through my hair.

"I don't have long. Remy still wants the shop open, if you can believe it, despite everything going on. I'll need to get back there soon, but I wanted to see you."

"I'm so glad you came." I crossed over to him. "I've been worried. Are you alright? I've heard about the riots."

He shook his head. "They weren't riots. Not until today."

I raised an eyebrow.

"I mean, people were upset. But it didn't get violent until now."

"How violent?" I dreaded his answer.

"About five or ten injuries last I heard, maybe even a death. I don't know for sure."

I bit my tongue and wondered for the thousandth time if Mother had been right all along. *Maybe everything would be normal if I'd just let Tor get demoted.* My shoulders drooped.

"Hey, hey, hey," he said. "You know this isn't your fault, right?"

"Maybe if I hadn't been so eager to go to the inspect—"

"If the circus of Tor's murder trial caused this, it's Tor's fault—and the king's, if we're being honest. Not yours. Tor killed someone, and the king let it develop into a spectacle. You just tried to set everything to rights."

Out of the corner of my eye, I saw George glance at us and then move to the door. "I'm going to pick up a few things from the shop," he called as he left.

When the door closed, I said, "You make it sound so black and white. Like I was just the hapless defender of justice. Like I had no selfish motivations when I went to the authorities."

He shrugged. "What? It wasn't like you were trying to get rid of your fiancé."

"No," I said. "I did like him. Before the murder, I thought I'd grow to love him, even. I was satisfied with the match."

"What made you turn him in?"

"I don't know," I said. "I was afraid, I guess. Panicked. It seemed like the only viable course of action."

"I think there was more to it than that," he said. "If you were making the decision only out of fear, I don't think you would have gone to the inspectors. What did you have to gain? It would never help your reputation. You would've known that Yvonna would see to that. You didn't need the notoriety—as Cleo's daughter, you already have the ear of the king if you ever need it. I think selflessness drove your actions."

I scoffed. "Maybe you don't know me as well as you think."

"I think I do." He floated in front of me now and tucked a strand of my hair behind my ear. His intense amber eyes bored into mine. "I remember a girl who wouldn't let the rich kids bully me at school, even when they made fun of her for protecting me."

"My social position was never at risk," I said. "The ribbing was all good-humored."

"Didn't always seem like that to me." He gently placed his hands on my shoulders. "You've always defended people. It was . . . attractive to me when we were younger."

"It was?" I whispered.

"Of course," he said, reaching his left hand out toward my cheek but drawing it back before his fingers caressed my face. "I mean, I knew you and I couldn't ever be a couple. It would've been scandalous."

I snorted. "Mother would've had your head."

"What do you think? Would it still be so scandalous, after everything that's happened?" His right hand trailed down my arm.

Heat rushed to my face. "What? Because my reputation's already damaged?"

He hesitated. "No, not like that. A cross-class marriage just looks silly and unimportant next to a murder."

I saw the truth written on his face, but I let it go. "You know as well as I do how insidious the gossip is in Thessalonike."

"Do you care anymore?" He pressed his forehead to mine.

"Don't take liberties." I pushed away from him.

"I'm sorry," he said, clasping his hands. "I thought you felt the same way."

I opened and closed my mouth. *Do I?* "Maybe I did, once. Before you left. But it's been a long time."

He looked down at the seafloor. "I respect your feelings."

"Alexander, it's not like that."

"Then what *is* it like?" His words were gentle, and disappointment and desire battled in his eyes.

"It's . . . the world is complicated. Especially right now. With everything going on in the naiad quarter. We'd have to leave Thessalonike."

"Why?"

"The mer would never accept it if I got engaged to someone I loved in school so soon after Tor's conviction. I—"

"So you did love me?" His eyes twinkled.

"No, I didn't—"

"You just said you loved me in school."

I glared at him.

"Jade, for me, there's never been anyone else. I know you have a lot more to lose in this than I do. I'm not risking anything but my feelings, and you're risking your whole world. So I understand if that's something you can't do, especially after so long. But I'd go to the ends of the ocean for a chance to be yours."

I almost smiled at him. "You haven't changed, have you? Always melodramatic."

"I prefer poetic." He winked. Then his smile faded. "I really thought I would change. I thought I could forget about you if I stayed away long enough," he said with a half-laugh.

"I'll think about it." I held his gaze for a long moment.

He drew my hand to his lips and kissed it. "That's all I ask for." He glanced at the tide glass. "It's time I got back to the naiad quarter. If the chaos dies down and customers show up, Remy will have my head for leaving the shop unattended."

"Stay safe." I squeezed his hand. "It would kill me if something happened to you."

"Then swim away with me."

I closed my eyes. "Please don't ask that of me again. Not until I've had time."

He released my hand. "You stay safe, too."

He opened the door, and with a final, lingering look at me, he propelled himself into the canal.

I stared at the wall in silence until George returned, carrying a basket of food.

"You could do a lot worse," George said as he unloaded the food, putting it into the cupboards. "Tor, for example, would've been a worse pick."

My head snapped up. "How did you know Alexander asked me?"

He chuckled. "Wasn't hard to read the look on his face, Miss Jade. I've had that same expression myself—lovestruck for a girl I knew I couldn't marry."

"Really? Who was that?" I scooted to the edge of the hammock, hooking my arms underneath my fin.

He looked rueful. "Do you really want to know?"

"Of course!" I said, a genuine smile overtaking my face.

"Lady Yvonna."

My mouth dropped open. "Lady Yvonna? *The* Yvonna?"

A hint of a smile danced on his lips. "This all happened years before you were born, in the days when Yvonna put her resilience and determination to better use than she has in weeks past."

"But . . . Yvonna?" I couldn't picture the two of them together in my head no matter how hard I tried.

"We attended school together. She was a year younger than I and a member of a family that ranked among the lowest in the hierarchy. But they were still a noble family and therefore leagues above me. She swore she loved me, but I think we both knew it couldn't last. When she received the marriage proposal from Felix, which vaulted her higher in the hierarchy than she ever could've dreamed, our mad romance came to an end." He shook his head. "Seeing what she's become, I suspect it's better that way."

"Maybe not," I mused. "Maybe if she'd made a different choice, she'd be a better person."

"Perhaps. Or maybe she's not as bad a person as you think her to be. Tor did a wicked thing, but he's still her only—"

The door banged open, and Mother swam in, irate, murmuring something about the *skub naiads* under her breath.

Benjamin followed behind her, his shoulders slumped. I looked at the tide glass and realized she'd pulled him out of school early. *That bad, huh?*

George shot me a pained smile. "We can talk about this

more later, if you want. Lady Cleo, may I be of assistance?" He floated toward Mother.

I decided it was about time I left the house. I didn't want to deal with Mother on the warpath, not with confusion about Alexander dominating my thoughts.

She began ranting to George about how her whole life's work of successfully adopting the naiads into the city was going to waste because of the riots.

Slowly and carefully, I scooted toward the door, hoping to slip out unnoticed. I itched to swim with Kiki.

"Jade, it's too dangerous out there right now." Mother shot me a sharp glance.

"I'm not going to the naiad quarter," I said. "But I really have to find Kiki. I've only been out there three times in the last month, and I'm sure she misses me."

She thrust her hands up. "Whatever. I probably couldn't restrain you if I tried. But stay the depths away from the quarter."

Despite everything going on, I couldn't stop myself from grinning, but I turned my head so she couldn't see it. No point in irritating her or making her think I didn't understand the severity of the riots.

I hoped Pippa and Miriam were alright. I wondered if William had gotten better. *Surely Pippa would've let me know if he was gone . . .*

And, of course, I worried about Alexander, too.

Anxiety churned in my stomach. I couldn't imagine how I'd answer Alexander. Clearly, I couldn't marry him. Not unless we left to make a fresh start as commoners in another city. Marbella, I supposed. It was the closest.

The mer in Thessalonike would think I'd staged the murder accusation—maybe even the murder itself—to get out of my engagement and marry my common lover who lived in the naiad quarter. Talk about a scandal that wouldn't go away.

I grabbed my father's cloak—I'd learned that lesson—and

bolted out of the house and toward the city gate. After about two blocks, I joined the murmuring throng of mer gathered in the canal.

*Another rally,* I realized. Andronicus, the same charismatic mer who had led the last rally, hovered over the crowd, working them up into a frenzy.

"The naiads think they can get away with setting up our most beloved captain of the guard for murder?" he yelled.

"Expel them!" someone shouted from the crowd.

"And now," Andronicus called, "*they're* protesting that they've been dealt with unfairly? They're rioting like the animals they are!"

My whole body went cold, and a sense of déjà vu disoriented me.

"Why isn't the king doing anything to check the naiads' power?" he yelled.

I didn't want to provoke a repeat of the last rally's events, so I darted down a culvert that connected to another canal. Any other canal. I didn't care where it took me just so long as I escaped from the rally and its insidious hate.

The culvert dumped me out into the canal that separated the city from the naiad quarter. My heart leaped into my throat. A deathly quiet hovered over the quarter.

CHAPTER

# SIXTEEN

*I need to get out of the city. Kiki needs to know I haven't forgotten about her. And I need space from all this madness.*

But almost as if by compulsion, I started across the canal toward the naiad quarter. When I got halfway across the canal, I stopped.

*I'm being crazy.*

I hesitated a second longer, then turned and flipped toward the city center so I could get to the city gates without going through the anti-monarchist rally. No need to complicate things further.

The guards at the city gate gave me a curt nod as I darted onto the open reef. I didn't see Maximus among them, and I hoped they wouldn't hassle me on my way back in.

Dismissing the thought, I soared across the coral gardens—pausing for just a moment to inspect the growth of a crimson-and-yellow plant I'd been admiring for a year—until I reached the spot in the reef where I usually met Kiki.

"Kiki?" I called. I clicked my tongue. "Come swim!"

She didn't respond, and a surge of panic raced through my veins.

"Kiki?" I shouted. *Please be here.*

I'd been absent from the reef for over a week. What if she'd thought I wasn't coming back? What if she'd moved on and joined a pod? I clicked as loudly as I could.

"Kiki!" I called again. Flicking my fin, I moved forward, away from the city in search of her. "Come here, girl!" My heart shipwrecked. I couldn't have lost her. I just couldn't have. I screamed, "Kiki!"

Seconds later, I heard a frantic clicking, and then Kiki surged through the water from the south and brushed up against me. I giggled, relief flooding my body.

"Hi, girl!" I said, wrapping my arms around her. "Oh, I'm so happy to see you."

She whistled.

"I've missed you, too. Let's swim."

I raised one hand above my head, and she sank downward to the perfect level for me to grab her dorsal fin. I scratched the spot I knew she loved, right behind her fin, and she surged forward, slicing through the water.

"Good girl," I cooed. Life inside the city wouldn't be normal again for a very long time, but at least I still had this.

She let out a squeal and arched her body toward the surface. A moment later, we broke out of the water into the warm, yellow sunlight. I squinted against its brightness, and we dove back into the waves.

When I readjusted my grip on her fin, she took off toward the deep ocean with me in tow. A thrill of excitement tingled throughout my body.

We darted through the cut in the reef, and I looked at the dark, forbidding water that extended hundreds—perhaps even thousands—of fathoms beneath me. It was colder here, and I'd start shivering if we stayed out too long. But defying conventions and embracing danger made me feel alive.

Something brushed against my fin, and I suppressed a little scream as I looked back. It was just a school of tiny silver fish, flashing in the light that pierced the water.

Kiki headed for the surface again, this time just long enough to suck in a breath of air, and then we plunged into deeper water. We never went far down—not more than ten fathoms or so—and we didn't stay down long, but I always loved this part of our swims.

"I don't know what to do," I said to Kiki as the water grew murkier. "There's something strange going on with Felix's business. Something illegal. I just wish I knew what it was."

She clicked at me.

"I know, I know. You don't like it when I'm stressed." I brushed my hand against one of the plants growing along the side of the cliff. "Ow!"

I drew my knuckle to my mouth and saw a jellyfish emerge from its hiding place in the seaweed.

Kiki squealed, and I thought I detected a hint of amusement in her tone.

"Shut up," I said.

She squealed again, lower this time.

I shook my head as she continued our descent. We'd descended deeper than usual, but I didn't make any move to rein her in.

Of course, we never ventured deep when anyone else was with us, not even Kora or Rhea, lest a report somehow get back to Mother. She already thought I took too many risks.

*And yet, being with Kiki is safer than swimming in the city canals these days.*

My stomach dropped at the thought of Rhea. But she'd made her choice, and I'd made mine.

Just when the cold became unbearable, Kiki turned back up toward the surface. Moments later, she broke through into the sunlight and air one more time, and then she started to make her way back to the reef.

I rubbed her belly. "Good girl. I wish I'd brought Pippa out to swim today. She wants to meet you, you know. But I don't know if she even wants to talk to me right now."

Kiki whistled.

"No," I said. "I don't think I'm going back yet. I'd rather stay out here with you today."

She blew bubbles out of her blowhole.

"Yeah." I planted a kiss on her snout. "I wish I was a dolphin like you."

We cavorted on the reef for another two hours, playing tag in the seagrass and riding the currents. I felt more relaxed and carefree than I had since that awful, awful party where everything fell apart.

"Lady Jade?" called a male voice from behind me.

Startled, I whirled around.

Maximus floated several yards away from me.

"What are you doing here?" I asked.

"I suppose I could ask you the same question," he said. "But I'm here to find you. The guards at the gate reported that you came out here several hours ago. The king would like an audience with you."

"Now?"

He nodded. "May I escort you back?"

"Yeah." My shoulders drooped. "Yeah, I guess."

I whistled at Kiki and patted her side. She rubbed her head on my shoulder and darted away.

"Why does the king want to see me?" I asked.

He shrugged. "I don't question His Majesty unless I need to know the answer."

"Fair enough." I envisioned the king's severe eyes and bushy beard. "I probably wouldn't either if I were in your position."

The corners of his mouth curled upward. "You ready?"

I cast one final glance in the direction Kiki had gone. "Yes," I said, swimming past him toward the city. "Let's go."

When Maximus caught up with me, he asked, "Do you often dance with wild creatures on the reef?"

I wrinkled my nose. "Kiki isn't wild. I rescued her when she was tiny."

"She isn't domesticated in the way the merchants' dolphins are."

I laughed. "No. I can't imagine her pulling a cart. But I try to come out and see her a couple times a week. Recently, it's been less often, of course."

We drifted into silence, but it seemed more companionable than I'd expected. After a lengthy period of quiet, right before we reached the city gate, he turned to me.

"I'm sorry I doubted your story. After hearing Rhea's testimony . . . well, the retraction of her testimony, I'm afraid I misjudged you. Misjudged the whole situation."

I looked down at the coral reefs below us. "I just wish none of this had happened. It isn't something I'm happy to be right about."

"The whole city shares your sentiments."

"Not the whole city." I gave a dark chuckle. "I barely avoided another of your brother's rallies today."

His eyes hardened. "Andronicus fancies himself a revolutionary. He's always looking for a new cause to use to stir up trouble. Really, he's just anti-monarchical. He opposes everything the king does because he wants to set up a new form of government. You know, the ideals of democracy and all that."

I shrugged. "I have no opinion on the question in principle. But it seems to me that the king is a fair ruler."

"I serve at the pleasure of the king."

"Would you want anything else?" I raised my eyebrows.

"You know how to ask dangerous questions. But no, I wouldn't. I'm committed to the great legacy of Thessalonike."

We passed under the arched gateway. The guards on duty glanced at us but said nothing.

"Do you think Tor's father is involved in illegal business dealings?" I asked.

"You really do have a talent for questions that could get you killed, don't you?"

I swallowed the lump in my throat. "So you do think something's going on?"

"Those sorts of things exceed my pay grade. But you could ask your little naiad friend. The sister of the girl who got killed. If the dead girl knew something, the sister might too."

*Yes, she does know something. Or at least she suspects something.* I couldn't fathom any other reason she'd go to such great lengths to hide the tablet.

Instead, I said, "We haven't spoken since the verdict and sentencing. She's grieving."

"Or afraid."

"Maybe that, too."

We turned onto the most opulent canal in the city. The palace lay at the far end of it, near city center. We swam in silence down the canal, and Maximus turned away from me as we entered the courtyard.

"The king is in the court," he said. "I must return to my post."

I rounded the corner to the court's entrance and stared at the doors as I summoned the courage to enter.

Steeling myself, I pushed open the polished obsidian doors and approached the king, who sat on his throne on the far side of the room. As I drew nearer, I realized he was scratching something on a tablet.

"Lady Jade," he said, "I'm glad you've come."

"I wasn't aware that I had the option, sir."

He chuckled. "No, I suppose not. But you must know that I don't rule by fear and intimidation."

"That is why your subjects love you, Your Highness."

He sighed. "Not all of them."

"Most of them, then."

"Perhaps not this week. The mer are angry that Tor was convicted without a witness to the act of murder, and the naiads are enraged that his sentence was so light."

"Aunt Junia called it a verdict to anger everyone."

"Your aunt is wise," he said, running a finger through his beard and staring at me.

"If it is not too forward of me to ask," I said, shifting my body, "to what do I owe the honor?"

"I have a favor to ask of you," he said, "for the good of the city."

I studied his face and quirked my eyebrow. "I can't imagine what position I could be in to impact the whole of Thessalonike."

"More than you know."

I dipped my head. "How may I be of service, Your Highness?"

"Sir Tor, as he's now known after his expulsion from the Royal Mer Guard, will soon extend another offer of marriage to you."

I blanched. *You can't be asking me to . . .*

"I was hoping you would accept."

CHAPTER

# SEVENTEEN

Silence stretched between us for a full minute.

"And why—" My voice had grown cold, but I couldn't help it. "—would I be compelled to do such a thing, Your Highness?"

"I hope you don't see this as a command, Lady Jade," he said, his voice deep and steady. "Your family has served this throne and this city too faithfully for that. Call it an opportunity to heal the city."

He pressed his fingertips together and peered out at me from underneath his bushy black eyebrows.

I clenched my jaw to stave off panic.

"As you know," he continued, "the naiads are rioting. The mer are calling for their expulsion from the city. There is fighting breaking out in the canals."

I swallowed and looked down at my hands.

"Much of this could be mitigated—eliminated, even—if you announced the rekindling of your engagement to Sir Tor. His connection to your family would ensure the continuation of his own position in society."

"Be so good as to explain to me, Your Highness, how this solves any of the violence in the canals?"

"It would be a symbolic way to assure the mer that their way of life is not threatened by those they see as interlopers. When they calm down, they will cease their continued persecution of the naiads. Eventually, the naiads will settle as the attacks in the quarter become less frequent," the king said. "Things can return to normal."

"I've been led to understand that attacks in the quarter have been going on since the naiads arrived a decade ago."

He tilted his head. "You and I both know they've intensified since all this began."

"What if you're wrong? What if it doesn't help?"

He gave me a bemused smile. "You're a lot like your mother. I firmly believe the violence against the naiads will abate if Tor can resume his place in society. The rabble in the canals will be forced to regroup and come up with something new with which to foment malcontent. That gives time for tensions to mend, if not heal."

"You're putting a lot on the shoulders of a single mermaid. And if I refuse?"

"I will not speak another word of it, good or bad."

I stared past the king at the walls of the court. A carving of the warrior queen Eliana caught my eye. *Be brave,* she seemed to say.

But what was *brave* here? It seemed so clear-cut in the histories.

"There is something else you should know," the king said. "The naiad William died last night of the injuries he sustained in your canal."

I froze. The room spun around me.

"His sister tried to bring him back to the house of healing when his condition deteriorated. Perhaps he could have been saved. But with the tension in the city, the physicians were afraid to let a naiad in."

"The naiads are being denied medical care?" My voice squeaked.

"When I heard of the situation, I forbade them to deny entrance to the naiads. Too late for William, I'm sorry to say. Your mother said he was a friend of yours."

"Yeah." I swallowed, struggling to keep my voice steady.

"I mean, I didn't know him well. We met after Anna's murder."

"Tell me about him," the king said softly.

I stared at the floor. "He was in love with Anna. After Pippa's house was attacked and vandalized, he rebuilt it so her landlord wouldn't come after her. She couldn't pay him anything, but he did it anyway."

The king tilted his head toward me. "Then you understand the stakes."

My fingers tingled. *He's wrong. He has to be wrong.*

"Take some time to consider it." He waved his hand at me. "I understand that it's overwhelming."

"That's an understatement," I said, my voice quiet.

"You are dismissed."

I turned around and fled from the court and the palace as fast as I could, trying to outswim the fear that clung to me.

I TORE through my front door, still shaking all over.

Mother jerked upright. "Jade? What's the matter?"

I began sobbing before I could get out the first word. In broken sentences, I managed to convey the king's request.

Her face was blank when I finished.

"D-d-did you know?" I demanded.

"Of course not, my dear," she said, drawing me into a hug. "I would never have let him suggest it to you." Her expression hardened. "That must be why he sent the advisors home early. He knew I wouldn't tolerate it."

"Is he r-right? Would an engagement between Tor and me put everything to rest?" I started to regain control of my voice, but turbulent emotions still stormed in my head.

She looked at her hands. After a long time, she said, "It's

not your problem to remedy. I won't have you marry a monster in hopes that it might quell the conflict."

I looked her in the eye for a moment before I softly said, "That's my decision, not yours."

She stiffened. "Jade, don't throw away your whole—"

"I haven't made a decision yet."

"Your father wouldn't want you to marry him under duress like this."

"Father would want me to be brave. Whatever that means. He knew about self-sacrifice."

"Jade—"

"He knew the risks," I said, my voice tight, "when he went to try to negotiate with the liberationists."

She grabbed my arm. "Stop being melodramatic. Our family has suffered enough already. We've given up a lot for the city. Do you think for a moment that Tor will ever forgive you, even if he marries you to save face? Your *life* might be in danger."

"I'm not a battered woman who can't give up her lover. You know I'd never marry Tor if the stakes weren't so high. I just want the hate and violence to stop. Before more people die."

"Is this about William?"

"It's about everyone."

"Do you really think you're so significant in this?"

"The king seems to think so."

"The king is a fool," she spat with venom in her voice.

I drifted backward, startled. I'd never heard her criticize the king.

Glancing at the corridor, I wondered if Benjamin was in the house or still at school. I didn't have a clue what time it was. I hoped he was at school; I didn't want him overhearing this conversation.

"Don't fancy yourself a martyr, Jade. If you marry Tor and any harm befalls you, we'll be no closer to peace than we are now."

"If he kills me, he's the fool. He might be able to get away with murdering a servant—especially a naiad—but to kill your daughter? A high-ranking noble? One of the king's favorites?"

"You underestimate the motivating power of rage."

I remembered Father's funeral. The moment we'd floated on the edge of the reef and cast his body to the depths. The white-hot anger that coursed through me, and how I'd wanted nothing more than revenge.

But, over time, grief fades. And so did my lust for vengeance.

Kiki hadn't understood why I'd wanted to stay away from the drop-off after that, for almost a year. But eventually I went back. In a way, I felt close to Father out there.

And somewhere in the midst of it, I'd realized that Father wouldn't have wanted me to carry that blinding anger against the naiads—or even the liberationists. He'd chosen to risk his own life to try to set the city right. He'd preferred to die than to hate.

"I don't know what I'm going to do," I said. "But I'll hear him out, at least, when the time comes. He's under house arrest at his parents' home for the next year, so a marriage can't occur until he's served his sentence. Perhaps he and I can agree to announce an engagement and then quietly back out once things have settled. That might serve both our purposes. I can't imagine he really wants to marry me any more than I want to commit myself to him."

My mind flashed to the tablet that Pippa had hidden in my wrap. I wondered again what was so important about it.

I looked at Mother. "I'm sorry that I can't promise what you want to hear."

Her voice had settled into an even tone. "If you want to get yourself killed, I suppose that's your business."

"Your passive-aggressive protest is duly noted."

She glared at me.

"I'm sorry, Mother."

She remained silent.

"I'm going out," I said at last. I swam for the door.

"You'll be letting him get away with it," she said just as I opened it.

I paused on the threshold. "What?"

"If you marry him or agree to an engagement so that everything can go back to the way it was. You'll be letting him reclaim his old life, ensuring he suffers no lasting consequences for the murder. That is neither brave nor just. Don't mistake a desperate desire to salve your conscience for bravery."

My hand trembled on the doorknob. "I'll think about it."

I fled into the canal.

My emotions were spiraling out of control again. Where could I go? *Aunt Junia's?*

I shook my head. She wouldn't rest until she found out what was bothering me, and I didn't want to talk about it. She'd react the same way Mother had.

*Alexander's?* My heart sank into my stomach. *Definitely not. Not when I'm thinking about getting engaged to Tor.*

I turned down the canal, hoping Andronicus's rally had dispersed.

*Pippa,* I decided. I'd go see if I could find Pippa.

I hesitated for a moment. Entering the naiad quarter wasn't the wisest idea, but it had seemed quiet enough earlier, before I went swimming with Kiki. Besides, I didn't know where else to go. *Oh well.*

THE SOUND of shouting somewhere off to my left drew my attention as I swam deeper into the naiad quarter. It sounded like a clash between mer and naiads, and I didn't want to swim into it.

I'd have to swim a little out of my way to get to Pippa's, but that seemed a far better option than darting headlong into a riot. I wanted to scream at the mer who had invaded the naiads' territory, but it wouldn't do any good.

*Just focus on what you can control.*

I hurried down the canal and broke off to the left when it seemed like the raucous shouting had faded. I managed to arrive at Pippa's without attracting any attention.

When I found myself staring at her door, panic strangled me. *This was a terrible decision. What if she doesn't even let me in? Clearly she doesn't want to talk to me right now. She's been avoiding me for days.*

I visualized the tablet she'd sewn into my wrap. I had to figure out what Felix was doing before I made any decisions about the king's request. I rapped on the door.

Shuffling sounded inside the house. Then Pippa called out, "Who is it?"

"It's Jade."

She unbolted the door and swung it open. "Get inside," she hissed. "What are you doing here?" She dragged me inside and closed the door.

"I needed to see you," I said.

"It's dangerous around here today."

"I need to know what you know about Felix."

She studied her hands. "What makes you think I know anything?"

"You know I like that gray wrap."

She cast a ball of shimmering water and ran it between her fingers. "I didn't think you'd find it so soon."

I raised an eyebrow.

"I hid it there knowing you'd find it. Eventually. The truth needs to come out. But the truth can wait a bit," she said. "Until things calm down. Until we have more to go on.

Sewing it into a wrap seemed like the best way to keep it hidden for a time. Your home is more secure than mine."

"Why didn't you answer the king's questions in the trial?"

She twisted her hands together. "If Anna was murdered over the tablet . . . it just didn't seem like I should talk about it publicly yet. The tablet was vague, and if we can't prove anything . . . I was just going to get myself killed by bringing it up."

"Why is Cassian looking for it?"

"Cassian?" She wrinkled her nose. "Do you think that's why he attacked you?"

"He ambushed me in my house, looking for it. He knew you'd hidden it there. He said his employer wanted to expose Felix."

Her eyes widened. "That's serious."

"You're telling me."

She shrugged. "I have no idea who he's working for or how they're involved. I didn't think anyone knew for sure that I had it. Anna smuggled it out of Tor's house shortly before . . . before he killed her."

"Do you know what it's for? It can't really be about pearls. It wouldn't be important."

She tightened her lips. "I know what Anna thought. But I can't prove she was right."

"Tell me."

"I think Felix is abducting naiads and selling them as slaves."

CHAPTER

# EIGHTEEN

Pippa leaned forward. "Anna said she'd stumbled onto something. That the timing of Felix's sales of single pearls to that overlander—his name is John something-or-other—always seem to coincide with disappearances in the naiad quarter."

"Disappearances?" I said slowly. My mind raced.

"We can't prove anything. Sometimes naiads decide to return to the river system in hopes that some of our people have survived. Or sometimes they venture too far away from the city and get caught by sharks or webbed-foot dragons—at least that's what we say among ourselves. The inspectors have never found any evidence that anyone's been taken . . ."

Dread curdled in my stomach. "But you think Felix is selling the missing naiads to an overlander?"

"I don't know if this John is really an overlander or if he lives in Marbella or even Thessalonike. But Anna had seen one of Felix's servants—a mer—lurking in the naiad quarter on several occasions. She thought it seemed like he was watching our friend Charlotte, and shortly thereafter she disappeared. She'd left a note saying she couldn't stand the saltwater any longer and hoped to find a livable river system. It wasn't like her. She didn't complain about the salt any more than the rest of us."

I rubbed the back of my neck. Then an even more horrific thought struck me. *Did Tor know?*

Even as I tried to push it away, the idea gained momentum, forcing me to face it.

*She was threatening my family,* he'd said. He'd tried to paint it as extortion gone wrong, but it hadn't rung true to me even then. *Why would he have killed her if it weren't true? If he could easily discredit her story?*

"She really got suspicious of Felix when she stumbled on those invoices. She just took the one, but she said there were five others that were similar, for one pearl each. And it didn't make sense to her because Felix made his money shipping large batches of pearls to the overlanders. There wasn't any reason for him to sell small batches, let alone one at a time. Maybe if he acquired a pearl of extraordinary value, but *six?* And all to the same buyer?"

"Maybe this John doesn't have the money to purchase a large batch."

"It's possible." She hesitated. "But Anna was killed over it." Her voice trembled, and I knew she was right.

I thought I was going to be sick. "Why didn't you go to the king with this after Anna's death?"

"With what? A stolen invoice and speculation?"

"The king is fair—"

"The king's position is precarious, and you know it."

I blinked. "No. I mean, it's not perfect, but he's a strong leader."

She rolled her eyes. "Really?"

"What?"

"You honestly think the king is in total control of the city? That he can maintain control if he defies the will of the most powerful mer in Thessalonike?"

"I mean, some of the nobles don't really like him, but there isn't much they can do about it."

She shook her head. "For the king to exercise power, he needs the support of the Royal Mer Guard. If that can be undermined . . ."

My hands felt weak. "I suppose we don't like to think about it very often. My family relies on the protection of the monarchy."

"You need other friends. Within the Guard."

"The Guard are loyal. Maximus protected me even when he thought I was lying about Tor."

"Who did he protect you from?"

"An angry crowd and . . ." I trailed off.

"And?"

"And other members of the Guard."

She nodded but said nothing.

"So, what you're saying," I said, my voice unsteady, "is that you didn't go to the king because you don't think he's powerful enough to take down Felix?"

*What the depths have I gotten myself into?*

"Maybe it could be done if Cassian's employer is a member of a powerful family. Assuming the employer really is against Felix, but we just don't know that. Cassian's employer could *be* Felix for all we know. Probably is, actually, because who else would know that a tablet was missing?"

"I don't want to imagine any of this," I said, avoiding her gaze by glancing at her home's drab furnishings.

"I don't either," she whispered. "But I don't have a choice. My sister is dead."

I massaged my temples and tried to calm the rhythm of my gills. My fins were clamped, and I couldn't seem to relax them. *What I wouldn't give for a dose of puffer fish tincture.*

"Why didn't you tell me all this earlier?" I whispered.

She shrugged. "It didn't seem like I should. Until we can get our hands on more proof, the fewer people who know, the better."

I remembered William and wondered if she'd heard about his death yet. From her demeanor, I doubted it. I wouldn't be the one to bring her that news.

"The king wants me to marry Tor," I said. "For the good

of the city. It makes sense if his power is waning. Why else would he go to such lengths to mollify Yvonna and Felix?"

Her eyes darkened, and her whole body stiffened. "He wants you to *what?*"

"That was my mother's reaction."

She shook her head. "Out of the question. Such a move would solidify the stranglehold that family has on the city."

*Because you're an expert in royal politics,* I wanted to snap, but I thought better of it.

Instead, I said, "I'm going to talk with Tor, at least. I don't think I'll marry him, but I might agree to announce an engagement that we quietly break off in a year. Maybe that will calm tensions."

Her nostrils flared. "Well, it's your life. But if you let him off the hook for his actions, Anna died for nothing." She clenched her hands.

"It isn't ideal, especially after everything that's happened, but—"

"I think you should go back to *your city,*" she said. "Have that chat with your precious fiancé."

"Pippa, what are you—"

She strode to the door and swung it open, her shimmery white dress swaying. "Be careful out there. Most people are staying indoors because of the riots."

I cast a long look at her. Then I bolted past her into the canal.

WHEN I RETURNED home, I was relieved to find that Mother had left. *Probably to confront the king.* Benjamin's schoolbag lay on the table, but he was nowhere to be seen.

As I floated up the winding coral corridor to my room,

I wondered if Pippa was right. Had we grown so reliant on our connection to the monarchy that we couldn't face the unpleasant truth that the king couldn't protect us forever?

I reached my room, opened a drawer, and pulled out the dolphin pendant that Father had given me. I clutched it to my chest, and my chin quivered.

"I don't know what to do, Father," I whispered. "You'd want me to be brave, but I don't know what brave is." I stared at my reflection in the ornate gold mirror on my dresser. "How do I do the right thing when I don't know what the depths is right in all this madness?"

*What would Alexander say?*

My throat felt hot and tight. I let my mind wander through a pool of memories. Moving to the window, I opened it and leaned my forearms against the sill. A gentle current flowed southward on our canal, and I bent forward to let it wash against my face.

Once, Alexander and I had gotten caught in a current while playing near the cut in the reef. *We must've been twelve. Maybe thirteen?*

Even then, I'd known better than to go off the reef without Kiki, but I'd overlooked the danger of a powerful rip current.

*"KIKI!" I SCREAMED as I flailed back toward the reef.*

*Alexander, a more powerful swimmer, had recovered and made it halfway back when he realized I wasn't with him. He turned back toward me.*

*"Go back!" I yelled. "It's dangerous!"*

*But instead, he surged toward me, reached out, and grabbed my hand.*

*"Go back," I said, pushing him away. "You can't pull me in. It's too strong."*

*"I'm not leaving you out here. Come on," he urged. "You can do this."*

*But I couldn't fight the current, and my heart raced faster and faster as it sucked us farther away from the reef.*

*"Let's swim sideways." He gestured to the left with his chin. "We need to get out of the current."*

*I nodded, turning so I was parallel to the reef and kicking my fin as fast as I could. We burst out of the current into calm, open water. We hovered over the depths in silence for a moment, and then, quivering, I threw myself into his arms.*

*"Shh." He wrapped his arms around me and planted a soft kiss on the top of my head. "We're alright. I can still see the reef."*

*"We—we can't get back through the cut." Sobs strangled my words.*

*"Not right now," he said, "but all that's left is to swim back to the side of the drop-off and hang out there just a little ways down from the cut. Once the current dies down, we slip back in, and your parents are none the wiser." He pulled back and tilted my chin up toward him. "Easy as can be."*

*I locked eyes with him, and a manta ray flipped in my stomach.*

*A shrill whistle resounded through the water, and I looked back in time to see Kiki burst through the cut in the reef and soar toward us.*

*With a half-sob, half-laugh, I swam toward her and wrapped my arms around her body.*

*She whistled again and turned toward the reef.*

*"Hurry!" I said to Alexander. "Grab on. She's going to tow us in."*

*We each wrapped an arm around her dorsal fin, and we swam back toward the reef, steering clear of the current until we made it almost all the way back. With a warning click, Kiki surged into the fast-moving water, and the three of us kicked as hard as we could toward the reef.*

*When we made it back to the field of seagrass, I collapsed to the sandy seafloor and reached out to take Alexander's hand.*

Smiling softly, I reached out and let the gentle current in the canal caress my fingers. Then I moved back to the mirror.

*I'm not a child anymore, and I have to think about what's best. Not just about what I want.* I set the dolphin pendant back in the drawer and straightened my back.

Above the waves, the sun was setting, and darkness descended on the city. It wouldn't do any harm one way or the other to hear Tor out, I decided. And the sooner the better. Before anyone else got hurt.

I twisted one of my most expensive wraps, made of jet-black fabric and adorned with diamonds, around my neck and over my body so it left my shoulders and the lower half of my torso bare. Then I slipped the dolphin pendant on underneath it so I could carry Father close to my heart.

I combed my hair but left it cascading down over my shoulders. When I looked in the mirror, I almost smiled. It was the perfect look to negotiate with status-conscious sharks like Tor and Yvonna.

I picked up a dagger Mother had given me for my fifteenth birthday—supposedly as a decorative piece but wickedly sharp—stared at it, and then tucked it into the folds of my wrap. I hoped the king would forgive my transgression if a situation arose in which I needed to use it.

I doubted he would. The use of blades except in times of direst communal need—like the siren invasion in the days of Eliana—ran contrary to our most time-honored traditions. Punishment was swift and severe, for the offender was judged to have placed their own welfare above the safety of the city.

*But I won't enter Tor's house without it. If I bring the wrath of the king down upon myself, I can flee to Marbella with Alexander.* A glimmer of hope lifted the tightness from my chest. *Better exiled than dead.*

Then a twinge of guilt nagged at my conscience. Maybe part of me was looking for an excuse to leave with Alexander.

After one more look in my mirror, I steeled my nerves and made my way down the corridor and out the front door, locking the door behind me.

When I turned into the canal, I caught Cassian staring at me from the corner. I held his gaze for a moment before I set off in the other direction toward Tor's house.

I didn't look back until I arrived on Yvonna's threshold, and when I did, Cassian melted into the crowd. I grunted as I rapped on the door.

By the time a servant—a merman, I noted—opened the

door, I had composed my face into a picture of calm. The servant invited me into the entryway and hurried off to inform Tor of my arrival.

For ten minutes, I floated alone in the entryway, and I wondered if Tor was making me wait to try to intimidate me. When he finally arrived, a wave of dislike rushed over me. I wanted to wipe the smirk off his face.

"Lady Jade," he said with an exaggerated bow and an affected drawl. "What a surprise. To what do I owe the honor of your presence?"

"Let's skip the pleasantries, shall we?" I said, forcing a smile.

"I don't see why not." He dropped his grin. "Why are you here?"

I glanced at the servant. "Can we talk in private?"

"Why don't we talk in the courtyard?" That smug grin hovered on his lips again, but the raw pain in his eyes tore at my heart. "I've so enjoyed our time there." He gestured toward the back door.

I set my jaw and swept forward through the door and into the courtyard. My eyes traced the bioluminaries on the courtyard wall and settled on the single, solitary seahorse at the feeder.

Tor followed me and closed the door behind us. I turned to face him.

"I have it on good authority that you're going to make me another offer of marriage," I said.

He scoffed. "And why would I do that?"

"To brush everything under the rug. Reintegrate yourself into polite society. It's so much easier to overlook a murder if we can all pretend it didn't happen."

He moved toward me. "Say your piece. Unless you've just come to try to insult me."

"No," I said, backing away. "I don't suppose I have." I fell silent, trying to decide how to begin.

He raised his eyebrows. "I'm waiting."

"Is my information good?" I asked. "Are you planning to ask again?"

"A marriage might benefit us both. I doubt I could stand to wake up next to your face for the rest of your life, though."

My hands went cold. "Is that a threat?"

He rolled his eyes. "Be real. You don't want to be stuck with me, either."

I thought of a lifetime shackled to Tor and grew nauseated. "I won't marry you. I can't."

"Then why are you here?"

"I'd be willing to discuss an engagement. Just for the public's benefit. We would quietly break it off in about a year."

"How magnanimous of you." He yawned and glanced at his mother's fire coral garden.

"You really did do it for your father, didn't you?"

He jerked his head back toward me. "What did you say?"

"I know that your father's hiding something," I said. "And you prize loyalty to your family and comrades above everything."

"What do you know about loyalty?" he asked, his voice tight. "We were getting married. We had committed our *lives* to each other."

I closed my eyes. "We were engaged, not married. But I didn't come to fight." When I looked at him again, he nodded for me to continue. "It's in your family's best interests to put this whole episode behind you as quickly as possible."

He kept his voice even. "If you think my father is involved in something he shouldn't be, why are you jumping at the idea of an engagement?"

"I want the violence to stop," I said. "There have already been too many deaths, and more people are getting hurt every day."

He snorted. "You can't put a tincture back in an uncapped bottle."

"I've heard rumors from a credible source that an

engagement between you and me would help pacify the mer. That they'd leave the naiads alone." I hesitated. "But I have one more condition."

"What?" he asked, rubbing the back of his neck.

"Your father stops kidnapping and selling naiad women."

He froze, his gaze locked on me.

I searched his face, and my heart fell. "You knew, didn't you?"

His jaw tightened, and he drummed his fingers against his cheek.

"Please tell me you tried to stop it," I whispered.

"Do you think I *wanted* any of this to happen?" he hissed.

"He can't be allowed to continue. We can fix this. He can buy back the naiads he's sold and set them free and swear not to do it again. I won't breathe a word."

Tor's gaze traveled downward to the floor, and he froze.

When he looked up, I didn't like the look in his eyes. I suddenly felt glad I'd brought the dagger.

"Ah, sweet Jade. Always the selfless one. Tell me," he said, clenching his jaw, "did you and Alexander become lovers before or after you sold me out to the inspectors?"

My forehead wrinkled. "What are you talking about? Alexander and I aren't—"

"Sure." He glowered. "You know, you could've just broken up with me when you decided you wanted out of our engagement. You didn't have to have me brought up on murder charges."

"I wanted out of our engagement the moment I learned that you'd killed Anna. I hadn't talked to Alexander in years. We reconnected in the naiad quarter when I went to pay my respects to Anna's sister."

He shrugged. "Whatever you say."

Fury roiled in my chest. "I'm offering you a way out of the depths to which you've plunged yourself, and you treat me with sarcasm and contempt?"

He lurched forward and grabbed my wrist. "You ruined my life," he hissed between his teeth, "and now you waltz into my parents' house and threaten my family?"

I held my head high. "You ruined your own life."

"Why the depths do you care so much about that naiad harpy? You should hate the naiads after what they did to your father. But you don't care whom you betray as long as you get your way."

I jerked my arm away from his grasp. "My father spent his life advocating fair treatment of the naiads. I'd betray his *memory* if I gave in to hate." My left hand wandered up to the dolphin pendant that lay underneath my wrap.

Tor lashed out and gripped me—one hand on my shoulder and the other on my throat. His fingers wrapped around my gills, and he slammed me up against the courtyard wall.

I struggled against his grasp.

"You know, Jade," he murmured. "I could ask you to marry me. We could announce our engagement, and everything could go back to normal. But so many people in the city hate you right now. So many people have motive to kill the little naiad-lover. Weren't you attacked in the canal the other day?" He chuckled. "Maybe I won't get my old life back this way, but it seems so much more satisfying to see your lifeless body thrown to the depths."

CHAPTER

# NINETEEN

M*y dagger.* I fumbled with my left hand in the folds of my wrap. *I need my dagger.*

Then I pictured Father's face as he left the house that fateful day to try to broker peace. *Always remember to be brave,* he'd said, then he'd squeezed my hand and swam out the door for the last time.

Tor constricted my throat and gills tighter, but that didn't seem nearly as important as the revelation I had in that moment.

*Father knew he might die that day, and he went anyway.*

My anger at Tor melted away just as I managed to grip the handle of my dagger, and I let my hand fall away without drawing it. I would make the choice that Father made. That the ancient Queen Jade had made.

*I would rather die than hate, even a skub like Tor.*

The water around me turned gray as my vision weakened. The dagger slipped out of my wrap and sank to the sand. Tor glanced at the blade and loosened his grip.

"Well, then, what did you bring with you? Did you plan to exact your own revenge?" He released me and shoved me down toward the floor.

My hands rose to my neck, and a deep soreness throbbed from my gills to my spine.

"I keep the dagger with me often," I managed to choke out. "You never know when you might come across thick kelp or overlander netting."

He grabbed the dagger. "I'm sure that's why. But I think the king might find it interesting, don't you?" He grinned. "I think taking this to the king might be even better than killing you."

"There's nothing illegal about carrying a dagger to cut kelp."

"You were planning to do a lot of kelp cutting in that pretty little wrap, weren't you?"

I fell silent. Talking hurt my throat, and it wasn't going to do me any good anyway.

"Yes. This is better. If I were you, I wouldn't even *think* about publicizing our little conversation. It'd be a shame if your brother had an unfortunate accident. I trust you can show yourself out. Don't try to snoop. Mother's home."

He left me crumpled on the seafloor, still rubbing my neck. A sob lodged in my injured throat, but I clutched the dolphin pendant and whispered, "So be it."

"JADE?" Yvonna closed the courtyard door and swam to my side. "What the depths are *you* doing here?"

I met her narrowed gaze and gestured to my neck.

She furrowed her eyebrows.

"Tor tried to kill me," I whispered.

She rolled her eyes. "Not this again."

"Tell me you can't see his fingerprints on my throat," I hissed.

She tightened her lips and eyed my neck. "I think it's time for you to leave."

I pushed myself up from the sand and floated upward. Every movement deepened the pulsating ache in my throat. "Do you know that your husband is kidnapping naiads and selling them as slaves?"

She started, squinting at me. "*What* are you going on about?"

"Your son confirmed it for me. It's the reason he killed Anna. She'd stumbled on it and threatened to expose Felix."

She lifted her chin. "Didn't you learn anything last time you spread lies about my family?"

"Why *did* your son murder Anna?" My voice croaked.

Her forehead wrinkled, but she recovered herself just as quickly. "You're asking the wrong person, I'm afraid, but if she was in the habit of chasing blackmail, I'm not surprised she got herself killed."

"Yvonna—"

"I'd hate for you to ask too many questions—you might find out firsthand why she died." She lazily traced her hand down her throat. "You really must be careful out there, Lady Jade. It'd be a shame if you met the same fate as your father."

"Please excuse me, Lady Yvonna," I said. "I don't associate with harpies."

I composed myself and drifted through the courtyard door into Tor's house, holding my head high so that the servant wouldn't see how broken I felt. With measured, even flicks of my feathery fins, I swam to the front door and into the canal.

I wondered if Tor would bring my dagger to the king directly or simply take it to the inspectors. I shrugged. *He's mad if he thinks the king will act against me for carrying a dagger.*

When I was halfway home, I started laughing—a frantic, hysterical laugh that sent a mother hurrying across the canal to shelter her small child with her cloak.

*Tor can't go to the king or to the inspectors himself. He's under house arrest. He'd have to send a servant.*

The servant who'd been on duty when I arrived hadn't seemed to be making any preparations to leave, so Tor was either making empty threats to scare me or waiting for a more dramatic moment to turn me in.

*Unless he's too worried the inspectors will discover Felix's slave trading during the investigation.* I moved forward again and admired a particularly vibrant blue tang. *Or maybe he wants the inspectors to haul me out of the house in the middle of the night.*

As my emotions flattened, I concluded he was delusional, though part of me wondered if I was being optimistic. After all, he only had to claim that I'd drawn the weapon on him—which I'd come quite close to doing, if I was honest—and the inspectors would have to investigate it.

Proving that I'd drawn the blade would be more difficult. Impossible, really, unless Yvonna or a servant claimed to have seen it. Especially since I had a bruised throat—or I would soon, anyway—and he didn't have a scratch. *If it comes down to my word against his, well . . . he's a convicted murderer.*

I shrugged. There wasn't anything I could do about it. I wondered if I should go to the inspectors to report Tor's assault on me.

When I reached the turn-off that would take me down to the inspectors, I swam resolutely toward my house instead. I wouldn't—*couldn't*—risk anything happening to Benjamin. And I didn't have the energy to answer the inspectors' intrusive questions, anyway. I couldn't even imagine explaining myself to Mother.

WHEN I OPENED the front door, Mother was sitting in her hammock at the table, resting her face in her hands. I slipped past, murmuring that I had a headache and needed to lie down, grateful that my wrap covered any bruising on my neck.

"Have you made a decision about the king's request?" she asked before I could float up the corridor.

I nodded, running a hand through my fuchsia hair. "You're right, Mother. I can't marry him. I can't even announce an engagement with the understanding that we'll break it off."

My voice was hoarse from Tor's grip around my throat, and I hoped she'd conclude I'd been crying.

*He'll kill me if I keep him close. Just like he killed Anna.*

The tension in her face seemed to soften. "Get some rest. You've been under a lot of stress, and a long nap is the best remedy for a headache."

I nodded and fled up to my room, but I didn't sleep. Though I felt numb, I couldn't quiet my racing thoughts.

A few minutes later, I heard Aunt Junia enter the house. "How's Jade?"

"Troubled," replied Mother in a soft voice, "but that's no surprise."

"She's in a very difficult situation. The king's request was hardly fair."

"She told me she can't marry him."

"Good," Aunt Junia murmured. "Has His Highness reached a decision about the riots?"

"A few of the naiads used daggers against the mer. And everyone is afraid of what the naiads will do if they are emboldened. If it came down to street fighting, the naiads' water-casting powers puts them at an advantage."

"You didn't answer my question," Aunt Junia said slowly.

"The king isn't ready to expel them yet, although some of the nobles are joining the rabble's cries for expulsion. Not many, though." She gave a tired laugh. "Generous of them, isn't it? When they rely so heavily on their naiad house servants?"

I couldn't quite make out Aunt Junia's response.

"But," Mother continued, her voice ragged, "I think it's safe to say that the naiads won't revolt again after they endure the king's wrath tonight."

*King's wrath?* I chewed my lower lip. *What does she mean?*

I wanted to bolt down the corridor and demand clearer answers, but I couldn't admit I'd been listening. I doubted she'd wanted me to hear any of it in the first place.

My heart pounded. Whatever the king had planned, the naiads needed to know about it. I wondered if it would affect the naiads hiding in their homes or if the rebels would bear the brunt of it. Maybe the naiads who'd killed Father would finally receive their due. Then I shook my head. Father wouldn't want justice like this. Not if it looked more like vengeance.

My whole body felt cold. I listened for a few more minutes in case Aunt Junia pressed for more information, but they shifted into a conversation about Aunt Junia's recent visit to the physicians.

"They say I'm just suffering from enervia," said Aunt Junia.

"Thank the tides," murmured Mother.

"Well, I suppose." Aunt Junia chuckled. "I mean, I'm glad I'm not dying."

"Can they do anything for the fatigue and pain?"

I glanced between my window and the curtain that connected my room to the corridor. I grabbed a cloak to wrap around myself, unhooked the shutters, and slipped out the window into the dim canal.

Whether Pippa wanted to talk to me or not, she needed to know that something big was coming. *Something the naiads will never forget.*

I QUIRKED my lips. *At this point, sneaking into the naiad quarter is starting to feel as natural as swimming with Kiki.*

I crossed the canal that separated the naiad quarter from the rest of the city, peering out from within the folds of my cloak and scanning the empty canals.

I still heard shouting from deeper within the quarter, but I didn't see anything that seemed like an immediate threat. Not that it made a difference. I'd committed to warning Pippa no matter what. *And Miriam. And Alexander . . .*

I thought about Alexander, and a small smile danced across my lips. It had been an awful few weeks, and I'd do anything to go back and change the way things had turned out, but I didn't regret finding Alexander.

*I'd go to the ends of the ocean for a chance to be yours,* he'd said.

As I flitted from canal to canal, trying to avoid interaction with anyone, naiad or mer, I found I already knew my decision. I would choose Alexander and leave the city with him. We could go to Marbella, where nobody knew my name, and start again.

I could only imagine Mother's reaction. She'd tell me I was rushing things.

In a way, she was right. But I'd grown up with Alexander. It wasn't like I'd only known him the last few weeks.

*And there's not much left for me here in Thessalonike. I can't imagine I'll get an advisorship or even another marriage proposal after all this, especially not if I'm accused of wielding a blade against Tor.*

*Better to start over.*

Relief flooded me. Everything would be okay.

I rounded the corner into Pippa's canal.

"Jade?" a voice called from behind me.

I stopped swimming and whirled around. *Alexander.* "You scared me!" My voice had gotten a little stronger, but it still warbled from Tor's attack.

"Oh, sorry," he said. "I didn't mean to."

"I know." I grabbed his hand. "Come on. We need to get

off the canal. I think the Royal Mer Guard are coming to put down the riots. We have to tell the naiads."

His eyes widened. "Are you sure?"

I hesitated. "I think so. Yes. From what Mother said, I can't imagine what else it could be."

"Go down to Pippa's, explain the situation to her, and get out of here. I'll spread the word."

I clutched his hand more tightly. "I—I can't go home if you're in the canals warning people. I have to know you got back safely. Spread the word as fast as you can, and come find me at Pippa's."

He held my gaze and raised one of his eyebrows.

"And after all this, let's swim away together," I said. "To Marbella, maybe?"

A grin spread across his face. "Really?"

I nodded.

He stroked my wrist with his thumb, and a tingle shot up my spine.

"I'll find you at Pippa's." He drew me in close and ran one hand through my hair as he kissed me. A volcano erupted in my chest.

"Come as fast as you can," I whispered. "The Guard could arrive at any moment."

He released my hand, and I trembled as I turned away from him and darted down the canal toward Pippa's house.

# CHAPTER TWENTY

"What the depths, Jade?" Pippa demanded, arms crossed and face unsmiling. "It wasn't safe earlier today, and it's certainly not any better after dark. I told you to leave."

"The Guard are coming to put down the protests," I said. "Alexander is out warning the naiads he finds in the canals."

Her nostrils flared. "You're sure?"

"I don't know details. Just overheard Mother telling Aunt Junia. It's happening soon. Mother said that after the king was done, the naiads wouldn't ever revolt again. I'm scared they might not only target the rioters."

Pippa blinked at me a few times and held her head high. "I'll be back in a few minutes. Do you think you can get out of the quarter in time, before you're caught up in it?"

"I don't know," I said. "I can't leave until I know Alexander is safe."

"It's happening tonight?"

I nodded. "And sooner rather than later, I believe."

"So, we don't have time to get out of the city," she murmured. "We'll have to stay behind locked doors and hold on to hope. That's served us well so far, hasn't it?"

She chuckled. *Probably to keep from sobbing.*

"I'll be back with Miriam soon. Her door was broken yesterday by a gang of mer, shortly after William . . ." Pippa trailed off, tracing the edge of her ethereal dress.

"I heard," I said.

"Anyway, her house isn't secure. So she should wait it out here with us. When Alexander gets back, you two should get out of the quarter."

"We'll try," I said. "You should come with us. We can all go to my mother's house."

"I'll be back as soon as I can. Xander knows where to find you?"

"Yes." I set my hand on her shoulder. "Be careful, friend."

She faltered a moment. "You too. If things go badly tonight, I'm sorry."

I chuckled. "And if things don't go badly?"

"Then I'll stay angry a little longer," she said with a wink.

"Well, then I hope we don't make up just yet." I smiled.

She squeezed my hand. "I'll be back."

After she closed the door, I tried to fight my rising panic, swimming back and forth from one end of the house to the other.

When that didn't work, I ran my hands along the walls and sparse furnishings, trying to focus on how the different textures felt against my fingers. Maybe if I could shift my attention away from the sounds of shouting seeping through the cracks around the door, I wouldn't worry so much.

I don't know how much time passed before Pippa returned—it seemed like hours, but I was too distracted to tell for certain. The key turned in the lock, and she spilled through the door with five naiads in her wake.

I recognized Miriam among them and Juliana, the water dancer who had mesmerized me. I vaguely remembered meeting the other three on the day Pippa had shown me around the quarter.

"The Guard are moving into place. We saw a whole battalion slinking through a canal. Is Xander not back yet?" Pippa asked when she saw my clenched hands.

I shook my head, and my gills flared.

She walked over and rubbed my back. "Xander is the most conscientious person I know. I'm sure he just wants to make sure that everyone knows. He'll be back soon."

"But if the Guard are already here—"

"Then there's nothing we can do about it," she said. "Here. You know Miriam, of course."

I nodded.

"And you might recall meeting Juliana, Sara, Quentin, and Westin."

"Yes." I tried to steady my voice. "It's very nice to see you all again."

"If only it were under better circumstances," said Sara. Her curly brown hair was pulled back into a bun, and her lovely, oval face looked tired.

I glanced around the room. We *all* looked tired.

I opened my mouth to reply, but pounding on the door interrupted me.

"Pippa! Jade!" Alexander's voice called.

I closed my eyes in relief as Pippa rushed to let him in.

"They're here," he gasped as she closed and locked the door behind him.

My eyes flew open and stared at his anguished expression.

"They're sweeping through the quarter, arresting anyone they catch out in the canal. One naiad shot a harmless plume of water at them to give himself an extra moment to get away."

"Foolish," I whispered, swimming toward him.

He nodded, agony etched across his face. "They killed him with their clubs. Right there in the canal. I don't think he was more than thirteen."

I reached out and took his hand. "I'm so sorry you had to see that, Alexander."

"Don't be," he muttered. "Be sorry it happened."

I moved backward like he'd slapped me in the face.

"No, I'm sorry," he said, reaching for my hand. "I didn't mean for it to sound that way. I just . . ."

"You don't have to talk about it," I said. "We just have to get through the night. We're stuck here. There's no way we can get out of the quarter without getting caught up in that mess."

"They're going into some of the houses, too," he said, "belonging to naiads they believe to be troublemakers."

"They won't come here," said Pippa. "Not unless they're loyal to Felix."

"Some of them might be," I said. "Tor was popular in the Guard."

"Well," she said, tightening her lips, "we'll just have to wait and see. Let's not use any light tonight. No need to draw attention to ourselves."

She covered the bioluminaries on the walls with a black curtain, and we sank to the floor in the darkness. Alexander's strong arms wrapped around me, and I leaned into the crook of his neck.

Screams sounded in the canal outside, and we stiffened, listening for any signs of the Guard. I squeezed Alexander's hand and prayed for it to end, but it kept going on and on and on.

"Do you remember your twelfth birthday?" Alexander murmured in my ear.

"That was a happier day," I said, the smallest smile playing at the corner of my mouth. "Mother was so angry with you when she found the puffer fish in the shell of kelp. It puffed up when she opened it and scared her to *death*."

"That was one of my more inspired moments. But that's not what I remember most about the day."

"What do you remember?" I asked, running my hand along his forearm.

"You were wearing a garland of shells in your hair, and you just looked so beautiful. And all of a sudden, I knew I was in love with my best friend."

Another scream sounded in the canal, this one close to the house.

"Say something, please," I whispered. "Anything."

"What do you think Marbella will be like?" he asked.

"Better than this, I hope."

"It couldn't be worse," he said with a dark laugh.

"Aunt Junia says there's hate in every city. In every person, really." Numbness crept over my entire body. "Maybe we can't escape it no matter where we go."

He held me tighter. "We'll figure it out—together."

None of the Guard tried to enter the house, and we held each other in silence until dawn.

BY THE TIME sunlight began filtering into the city, silence hovered over the naiad quarter. Alexander had fallen asleep with his arms around me, and I didn't want to disturb him by moving.

Everyone else had fallen into an uneasy slumber at some point during the night except for Pippa, who sat still, awake but looking at nothing in particular.

"I guess you still get to hold that grudge against me after all," I whispered.

She chuckled. "I guess so."

"I'm not going to marry Tor. Or even pretend that's the direction things are heading. No matter how the king tries to pressure me."

With a half-smile, she gestured at Alexander. "I think you'd disappoint someone if you engaged in that charade."

"I think I would," I said, rubbing his arm. "After things have had a chance to settle down—in a month, maybe two—we're going to swim off. To Marbella, I think. Or maybe one of the seven kingdoms beyond the drop-off. No one would follow us there."

"Maybe I'll come with you," she said. "I've heard that naiads and mer and sirens and kelpies all live alongside each other in Marbella."

"I don't know if it's true or not," I said. "The merchants who travel back and forth don't talk about it much, but it'd be wonderful."

We sat in silence for another few minutes.

"Why didn't the naiads go to Marbella to begin with?" I asked. "Why stop in Thessalonike if there are already naiads in Marbella?"

She stared at her fingernails. "Marbella was farther, and the journey had already been hard. The king assured us we'd be welcome, that the city would benefit from our ability to manipulate water. By the time we realized the truth, we were already settled here in the quarter. It's easy to move on when things are so bad that you can't stand them anymore. It's harder when they're just mediocre.

"Besides, what if Marbella isn't actually any better? What if they started worrying about our magic and wanted to sequester us just like you did? We're river creatures, and we float with the current, but that doesn't mean we want to wander endlessly."

"No," I said, staring at the latched window, wondering what lay beyond it. "I don't suppose it does."

Alexander shifted, and I slipped out of his arms.

"Is it alright if I open the window?" I asked Pippa.

She nodded. "It sounds like everything's settled down now."

I wriggled out of Alexander's arms, flipped over to the window, unhooked the latch, and pulled the shutters inward. My hand flew to my mouth. A half-dozen bodies littered the canal.

CHAPTER

# TWENTY-ONE

"What is it?" Pippa asked.

My voice croaked when I tried to answer.

Alarmed, she stood up and rushed to the window. She let out a shriek, awakening the others, who crowded around us. For a long time, nobody said anything.

The bodies were all naiads. One was a child. I clutched my stomach.

Alexander rested his hand on my shoulder. "It's time to go," he finally said. "You need to get back home. Your mother must be worried."

"She might not even know I'm gone," I murmured. "I lay down early pleading a headache."

I couldn't think about anything except the scene in front of me. *Who killed them? The Guard? The liberationists?*

My gaze lingered on the child's body. I thought about Mother's claim that the naiads would never revolt again.

*Was this planned?*

And then came the worst thought of all—

*Did Mother know?*

"He's right," Pippa said, her voice flat. "You should get out of here. You too, Xander. Stay away from the quarter for a few days. I—I can't imagine the aftermath of this will be good. The liberationists . . ."

I turned toward her. "Come find me later today or

tomorrow if you can. I want to know what really happened, not just whatever story the Guard feeds to the city."

"I'll try. If they're letting naiads out of the quarter."

"Tell them you're picking up some mending from my house," I said. "That should get you through. The nobles would throw fits if the naiads weren't allowed in to conduct their errands."

Pippa pursed her lips. "I'll do that. Stay safe out there, Jade."

Alexander floated next to me, fiddling with a string that had come loose on his wrap. His arms and face flushed red. "I can't leave the quarter. I don't have anywhere to go. My friends are all here, and—"

I placed my finger over his lips. "You'll stay with Mother and me until it's safe to come back."

"She can't—"

"And I'm going to tell her today that we're engaged. That is, if you'll have me." I gave him a sad smile.

His face lit up, and his protests died in his throat.

"Yes. Yes! Let's get married." He grabbed my hand, but his smile faded when he looked out the window at the dead naiads.

Pippa cleared her throat. "Okay, lovebirds. Get out of the naiad quarter before the liberationists start looking for blood. This won't be the only canal with dead bodies in it."

The rebuke in her statement stung more than I think she meant it to. She was right, though. It felt wrong to plan our future while overlooking the sight of a massacre.

*Would it have been any better if we'd been giddy before, in a city that didn't care if a captain of the guard killed a servant? Perhaps it's better to find joy in the rubble rather than celebrate in ignorance.*

We'd try again in Marbella. Perhaps we could make a new life together. And if not, it couldn't get much worse than the volcano our lives had descended into here.

I hoped the tides wouldn't take that as a challenge.

"COME AGAIN?" Mother sat at the table late that morning, her gills flaring. "You can't get *engaged*, today of all days."

Alexander and I held hands, uncowed by her fierce expression.

I'd slipped through my window shortly after sunrise. Alexander came to the door not long after and told Mother that he'd spent the night sheltering with Pippa and a few other naiads but leaving out my involvement.

"I'm already engaged," I said.

"If the city found out—"

"We don't have to announce it right away." I tried to keep my voice soft and reassuring. "We don't even have to announce it at all. I . . ." I trailed off.

Aunt Junia rubbed Mother's back. "Cleo, you need to relax for a moment. All the stress is getting to you. Would public opinion have kept you from marrying Augustus?"

I found my voice. "Mother, you said before the trial that you've come to respect me. Can you respect this decision? I swear I haven't arrived at it lightly."

Mother thrust her hands up. "Well, I suppose Alexander can stay the night. Pippa was right to send him here—it isn't safe for him in the quarter."

*There's my opening.*

"What did happen in the naiad quarter last night?" I asked. She didn't yet know that I'd gone there, and I hoped I could keep it that way.

She sighed. "The Guard went in. I knew they were planning to put down the riots . . . forcefully. But I don't think even the king himself was prepared for the result."

I raised my eyebrows.

"Over a hundred dead," she said.

Even though I'd seen hints of the massacre that morning, her words punched me in the stomach. "H-how? So many?"

She rubbed her temples. "I don't know. That was never the plan. There were supposed to be mass arrests. Maybe a few beatings. Not deaths. Certainly not on that scale. The captains went so far beyond their mandate that I can't even fathom it. Perhaps it was some twisted retribution on their part."

*Retribution?* The thought turned my gut. "What will the king do?"

"What can he do?" She scoffed. "Reprimand them formally and appear weak? Like he couldn't even control his own army? His pride wouldn't allow it even if everything else were simpler."

"So, they'll just get away with it," I murmured, my heart sinking.

"What did you expect? He was willing to ask you to marry a skub."

Alexander shot me a questioning look. I squeezed his hand and said firmly to Mother, "Well, it was wrong of him to ask. Besides, Alexander and I *are* engaged now, and we *will* be getting married."

Aunt Junia smiled at me, covering her hand with her mouth.

Mother shot her a sharp look. Then she waved her hand at Alexander and me. "We can talk about that later. Alexander, I'll have George make up the spare room in the back for you. Jade, don't forget that we're expected at Lady Regina's party tonight."

"I can't go to a fancy party," I exclaimed. "Not after hearing about what the Guard did to the naiads!"

She tightened her lips. "Regina should have canceled it. It's poor form to host a party on such a tragic day. But she did not cancel, and we must go."

"No." I folded my arms, and revulsion welled up in my throat as I thought about the bodies I'd seen in the canal.

"Jade," said Aunt Junia, "it's for the greater good."

I didn't say anything.

"I don't think you understand the political dynamics at play," said Mother. "For the family's sake—for your brother's sake as much as for your own—we have to take this step back toward normalcy. You don't have to stay at the party long. You don't have to enjoy yourself. But you must go and smile and start to ingratiate yourself back into the good opinion of the nobles."

"Alexander and I aren't staying in Thessalonike," I blurted out.

Alexander grimaced.

*Probably not the best time to make that particular announcement.*

Mother shook her head. "I don't have the energy to have this fight. Be ready for the party on time. You will visit with the most important guests for a full hour, and you will avoid any controversial . . ." Her eyes lingered on Alexander. ". . . subjects."

Alexander said nothing but kept his eyes trained on my mother. "Lady Cleo, may I speak?"

She sighed. "If you must."

"All of this must be as hard on you as it is on Jade. Perhaps even harder, given the great degree of responsibility you feel for advising the king appropriately. I know you take your duty seriously. And I know it isn't easy to hear that your daughter is marrying a man whose status is so far beneath her, especially when that means she's going to need to leave the city. But I want to do what I can to set your mind at rest. I've always loved your daughter."

"I know you have," Mother said, adjusting her necklace. "It's why I was so glad to see you leave school."

"Mother!" I snapped.

She held up her hands and cast me an innocent look. "What? I'm sure that didn't come as a surprise to him."

Alexander continued looking at her. "Lady Cleo, I would give my life to make Jade happy."

"I said we'll talk about this later," said Mother. Then she cracked a smile. "But at least it's a better match than the skub-whose-name-we-will-not-utter."

I glanced at Alexander and shrugged.

"Now," Mother said, "George is out on an errand, but he'll return in a few minutes to get you settled, Alexander. You'll stay here for a few days while everything settles down. I expect both of you to be responsible. There will be no eloping." She shot a stern glance at each of us.

I told her that I wouldn't make that kind of promise, but I would at least go to the party.

"Willful, headstrong child," she muttered. "Now get out of my sight, both of you. I have enough to worry about today without you children arguing with me at every turn."

Grabbing Alexander's hand, I led him down the hall to the sitting room at the back of the house.

As we moved away, Aunt Junia said to Mother, "She's a lot like you, you know."

"That's what I'm afraid of."

Alexander and I looked at each other, and I tried to suppress a burst of laughter. Then all my pent-up emotions ambushed me, and I collapsed halfway down the hall, sobbing.

"What's wrong?" Alexander sat at my side and looped his arms around my shoulders. "Are you okay?"

"No," I managed.

He rubbed my back with his hand.

"Everything's fallen apart," I whispered, "and I don't know how to process any of it."

"We've had a long night. Why don't you go up and try to get some sleep? I'll be fine down here by myself."

"I can't sleep," I said.

"Your eyes are bloodshot," he whispered. "It's a wonder your mother didn't realize where you'd been. You won't be able to get through that awful party tonight if you haven't at least rested."

He had a point.

"Alright," I said. "As long as you promise me you'll still be here when I wake up."

"Always." He kissed my cheek.

I squeezed his hand, floated upward, and made my way back past Mother and Aunt Junia and up the corridor to the second level of the house.

I swept into my room with a heavy sigh. My hands felt cold as I swam toward my hammock bed and sank into it.

"Are you okay?" Benjamin asked from my door.

I whirled around and took in his serious expression. "You heard my conversation with Mother?"

He nodded. "Of course I did. You're really leaving?"

My chin quivered. "I'm so sorry, urchin. If it weren't—"

He surged toward me and wrapped me in a hug. "Shh. I get it. You can't stay. Too much has happened."

"I just wish I could take you with us."

"Then Mother would *really* throw a fit," he said, moving back but keeping his hands on my shoulders.

I laughed and placed my hand on his. "Yeah, she would. I want you to know that I'm really proud of you. I've known for a while that you're growing up, but you've been so strong and supportive through everything that's happened, and I'll always be grateful for that."

"You're my sister," he said. "It comes with the territory."

I rolled my eyes and pushed him away. "Go away. I'm exhausted, and I have to try to rest before the party."

"I'm *so* jealous," he said with a smirk.

"Just wait about three more years, and you'll be stuck going to these things, too. They're awful."

"I bet the food's great."

"That is their one redeeming quality." I ran my hand through my hair.

He swam back to the door and stopped without turning back around. "Promise me one thing?"

"Anything."

"Don't leave without saying goodbye."

I wrung my hands together, glad he wasn't looking at me. "I promise."

"And stay as long as you can?"

"I'll try," I said with a catch in my voice.

MOTHER APPROVED of the clothes I'd put on for the party—a deep blue seaweed wrap that looked the part of elegance but didn't draw undue attention to myself and a simple strand of pearls.

When Alexander saw me, his ears tinted bright red. "You look beautiful."

"Thanks." I glanced down at the floor. Tor had been profuse in his compliments, but I'd never felt quite so giddy around him. *I suppose it's because I know Alexander means every word he says. With Tor, I never knew what was just politics.*

An hour later, Mother and I arrived at the party and greeted the hostess, Lady Regina.

"Cleo," she said warmly, grasping Mother's hands. "And Jade." She nodded at me, her eyes tightening, then she rushed away to meet the next guest.

My cheeks warmed, and I clenched my jaw. "Did you see that?" I whispered to Mother.

"Ignore it," she murmured. "Stay focused. Work the room."

I caught a glimpse of Rhea floating near the opposite wall. She glanced up from the lord she was flirting with—whom I knew to be married and guessed to be a full two decades her senior—and locked eyes with me for a brief moment.

I looked away. I couldn't bring myself to forgive her, and even if I eventually managed to let it go, I'd never trust her again. She'd broken too much between us. I turned and swam toward a group of girls I'd gone to school with.

"Lena, Angelica," I said. "It's been a long time."

They looked at me for a moment with raised eyebrows and swung back to each other, continuing their conversation as if I weren't there.

I realized then what was going on, and I turned away from them, brimming with anxiety and humiliation.

In a panic, I searched the room for Mother. I had to get out of there. I didn't particularly enjoy parties on the best of days, and I couldn't even imagine trying to mingle for an hour in a room full of people who hated me.

*Perhaps Alexander and I can leave for Marbella tonight.* I wondered if the people in Marbella would be any easier to talk to than the stuck-up, noble skubs of Thessalonike.

I saw Hera, one of my mother's friends, and decided to visit with her, at least for a few minutes. Whatever she thought of me, she wouldn't snub me in front of my mother.

"Hera," I said to her, "how are you?"

She turned her striking green eyes to me. "Why Jade, lovely to see you. I hope you've been well?"

"Very well, thank you. How are your children?" The stilted conversation agonized me, but at least I could pretend everything was normal.

"They are very busy, as always," she replied. "Oh, Vivienne just came in. If you'll excuse me, I have something quite important I must discuss with her. I hope we'll get another chance to visit later tonight."

"Yes, of course." My courage faltered. Vivienne had already been at the party when I'd arrived.

The buzz of conversation closed in around me. I would have to make my apologies to Lady Regina and claim I had a headache, regardless of what Mother said.

It wasn't like I really needed to reintegrate myself into polite society after the scandal. Alexander and I wouldn't be staying.

"Lady Jade," said a voice behind me. "*So* good to see you."

I twisted around to see Felix sneering at me. I threaded my fingers together.

"Lord Felix, what a *delight*." I didn't bother trying to sound sincere.

"I'm glad I ran into you tonight. I have great news. I knew you'd want to hear it."

The room spun around me. "What's that?" I asked with a pasted-on smile.

He pressed his hands together and grinned. "The king has agreed to expel the naiads."

CHAPTER

# TWENTY-TWO

My hands shook. "Come again?"

"Naturally, we can't have the naiads getting rowdy on us like they have these past days, now, can we? We'll be so much safer this way."

I crossed my arms over my chest, hoping he was bluffing. Surely the king wouldn't deport the naiads, least of all without consulting Mother. But something in me doubted.

"I've heard of no such plan," I said. "But, then again, Mother and I were in a rush to get here on time. It must have slipped her mind."

"Oh, I don't believe the king mentioned it to Cleo," he said in a dramatic whisper. "He can't very well tell a naiad-lover about it before it's announced in the canals, and your mother does have a record of being on the wrong side. Even after the naiads killed your father, she still wanted to protect them." He *tsked*. "Seems foolish, doesn't it?"

I looked over his shoulder and surveyed the room, locking eyes for a moment with a wide-eyed Yvonna. There was no one at the party I cared to have a conversation with and no point lingering to listen to Felix's threats.

"I must be going." I dipped my head. "I've made an appointment that I'm already late for."

I left the party with deliberate strokes of my fin and without a word to Regina or a glance at my mother.

"Lady Jade." Yvonna moved toward me as I reached the door. "Wait."

"Get out of my sight," I said under my breath. "And keep your dark, twisted family away from me."

"ALEXANDER!" I rushed into his arms upon returning home. He held me close, and we spiraled in a circle. "Oh, I'm so glad to see you. It was a terrible, terrible party."

*If I never see Felix and Yvonna again as long as I live . . .* But I felt a little infusion of strength at the thought that I hadn't let them smell my fear.

Alexander held me close, and I caught a glimpse of George over his shoulder. George tried to slip away down the corridor, but I called out to him. "George, I'm glad you're here."

George smiled at me. "I'm glad too, Miss Jade. I'm sorry you had such a foul evening."

"What happened?" Alexander asked in a low, soothing tone.

I bit my lip. "So many things. Everyone was rude to me. And then Felix said that the king's agreed to expel the naiads from the city."

George's eyes widened.

"I can't imagine that's true," said Alexander, his lips pursed.

"But what if it is?" My hysteria burgeoned. "I mean, maybe he was just trying to make me miserable, but what if it's true and my actions have really resulted in the expulsion of the naiads?"

"Hey, hey." Alexander ran his hands up and down my arms. "No matter what the king decides, none of this is your fault, remember? You didn't choose for Tor to kill Anna. You didn't choose to be the one who stumbled on the aftermath. You just told the truth."

My gills rose and fell rapidly, and I jerked out of his embrace and swam back and forth across the room.

"There's nothing we can do about it," he said.

"I could plead with the king."

"And say what? Do you really think he's going to change such a sweeping decision at the whim of a seventeen-year-old girl? No matter how much he respects your mother, if he's agreed to such a plan, it's irrevocable."

Nausea churned in my gut. "What if I agreed to marry Tor?"

Alexander pulled back. "What?"

"No," I shook my head, "not really marry him. Just be engaged for a while."

"What the depths are you talking about?" His nails pressed into his palms.

I pressed my lips together and shot an imploring glance at George.

Rubbing my temples, I said, "I should've told you this already, and I'm sorry. Yesterday, before the Guard swept through the quarter, the king requested an audience with me, and he asked me to marry Tor to help calm the mer."

"And you're *considering* it?" Alexander looked from me to George in disbelief. "What about us?"

I slammed my hand against the table. "Don't you think this is bigger than you and me?"

"If I may interject," George said.

"Yes?" I turned toward him. "You've always given me excellent advice."

"First, it's too late for an engagement to make any difference. The problem now isn't that the mer are restless. The Guard took things too far. The king is trying to stave off a full-fledged revolt in the naiad quarter. Don't imagine for a second that the anti-monarchists aren't trying to figure out how to press this to their advantage."

"That makes sense," I said in a thin voice. "What do you think will happen?"

George sighed. "I wish I knew, Miss Jade. Probably nothing much that will affect you or me." He pressed his fingers together. "Worst-case scenario, though, we could be looking at a revolution. That doesn't strike me as the likeliest outcome, but it would be foolish to discount the possibility. It's happened before."

"Not for centuries." I risked a glance at Alexander. His eyes still blazed at me.

"You kids are planning to leave, aren't you?" George asked, a hint of sadness shadowing his deep gray eyes.

"Yes." I rubbed the back of my neck. "How did you know?"

He smiled at me. "Because I planned to elope with someone once."

I reached out and grasped his hand.

He squeezed my fingers. "And a little fish named Benjamin hinted at it."

"Oh, depths," I said. "Is he here? I didn't want him to hear all this."

"He's at Niko's. But don't worry about him. He's a strong young man. Anyway." He cleared his throat. "As I was saying, you have friends among the naiads, Miss Jade. If you and Alexander need to leave Thessalonike to be together, travel with the naiads until they find safe waters. You don't have to take this journey alone. And you may be able to help keep them safe along the way. Marbella might prove more welcoming to them if there are mer in their midst."

Peace spread through my core. "Thank you," I whispered to George. "You always know the right thing to say. I—I don't know what I'll do without you."

"I sure will miss you, Miss Jade," he said, and his lower

lip quivered. "You and Benjamin and your parents have been like family to me for many years now."

"There isn't much that I worry about missing when I think about leaving the city. It's just you and Mother and Benjamin and Aunt Junia." My heart sank. "And Kiki."

"Kiki will come with you. Her whole heart belongs to you."

I knew he was right, and a weight lifted off my chest.

"I'm so sorry I have to leave," I said.

"Ah, I understand, child. When the time comes, I expect you won't have the chance to find me to say goodbye, so know that I'm very proud of you and wish you all the best. Your father would be proud of you, too. You've honored his memory in the way you've lived these past two months."

I smiled at him even as I thought my heart might break. "Thank you."

"Now," he said, steadying his voice. "Are you children hungry? What can I make you to eat? I assume you left the party before the food came out, Jade?"

I turned toward Alexander. "I'm sorry. I panicked. Forgive me?"

"You weren't . . . really considering marrying him, were you?" A frown still darkened his face.

"No! No, never," I said, reaching for his hand. "I just thought—for a moment—that we should think about postponing our marriage, for the good of the city. To help everyone calm down. I love you."

His jaw relaxed. "I love you, too."

George coughed.

"Oh, I'm sorry," I said. "Food would be lovely. Do we have crab poppers?"

"Always," George said with a bow.

EARLY THE NEXT morning, Alexander and I floated through the city, hand-in-hand, not caring who saw us in those few stolen moments. Only the workers were awake and moving about the city anyway.

Well, and the Guard, who maintained a heavier-than-normal presence in the canals.

We made small talk about sights on the canal for a few minutes, until I finally murmured, "I think George is right. We should leave with the naiads if the king expels them."

"Yes." Alexander gripped my hand tighter. "My home has been with the naiads for years now. I have friends among them. They'll welcome us."

"I'll tell Mother and Aunt Junia and Benjamin before we leave. And maybe Kora. But I don't think anyone else will miss me much."

He rubbed my wrist with his thumb. "Then they're foolish. And I think you should say goodbye to Rhea."

I froze, hovering in one spot. "Why?" I asked in a strangled voice.

"Because you might never see her again," he said. "You ought to try to set things right."

"I have no interest in speaking to Rhea again as long as I live." I pushed my father's face from my mind. "Besides, she certainly won't care. She made that perfectly clear. If anyone needs to set things right, it's her."

"She did an awful thing." He brushed his fingers across my cheek. "But I'd hate to see you leave the city without having at least tried to—"

"I don't want to." A blue tang moseyed past my face, and I focused on it to avoid making eye contact with Alexander.

He held up his hands. "Alright. You don't have to." He glanced in the direction we'd been swimming. "We're almost to city center."

"I'd like to spend some time looking at the statues. That's another thing I'll miss about Thessalonike." We started at the statue of King Poseidon, the first monarch of Thessalonike. His sage eyes looked down on me with equal measures compassion and reproach, like a loving father and a stern judge all in one. One by one, I moved down the line, saying goodbye to the city one piece at a time.

When I reached the statue of Eliana, I found myself face-to-face with Cassian.

CHAPTER

# TWENTY-THREE

"You frequent city center?" I asked Cassian.

"Not usually."

"Are you here to chase me down and demand things that don't exist?" I crossed my arms.

"What's going on?" Alexander asked.

Cassian's navy hair waved in the current. He ignored Alexander and addressed me. "No. I have it on good authority that you're eloping and leaving the city soon."

I glanced at Alexander. "Word spreads fast. Maybe I didn't need to tell my mother after all."

Alexander smirked at me. "I'm sure the conversation would've gone better if she'd heard it from someone else first."

I sighed. "What is it, Cassian?"

"My employer would really like that tablet, Lady Jade, if you have any ideas on where it might be."

Alexander looked from Cassian to me. "Would someone please explain *something* to me?"

I squeezed his hand. "I'll tell you when we've left the city. Trust me."

He rubbed the back of his neck but nodded.

I turned to Cassian. "What's on this mysterious tablet?" I phrased my next words carefully. "I still haven't figured out what Felix would be so desperate to hide."

"My employer believes it is the reason Anna was

murdered. If Tor was willing to kill for it, it suggests that it is damaging to his family."

I squinted at him. "You know more than you're saying."

He chuckled. "In my line of work, that's always likely."

Alexander grunted.

I raised my chin. "Perhaps if you could reveal who your employer was, I might be more inclined to speculate as to where such a tablet might've ended up."

He gazed at me. "If you want to do right by the naiads, you won't leave the city without handing over the tablet. Felix is selling naiads, Lady Jade. And the king cannot move against him without proof."

I pursed my lips. "Are you saying that the king is your employer?"

"I am not."

"How do I know you're not working for Felix?"

He hesitated. "It's a fair question, I suppose." His gaze darted to Alexander. "Suppose I tell you—"

"Thus says the king!" a crier's voice interrupted him. "In order that justice be served in the face of the uprising in the naiad quarter, sanctions are hereby handed down on the naiad population in Thessalonike."

Alexander and I looked at each other, our brows furrowed.

*Sanctions? Not expulsion?* Felix had just been trying to torment me after all, I decided. I wasn't surprised. It was just the sort of thing he'd relish doing.

The crier continued, "From this day and for a period of one year, a curfew shall be enforced in the naiad quarter. Any naiad found in violation of the curfew while within the boundaries of Thessalonike shall be subject to a fine of twenty drachmas. Naiads shall not gather together in groups of more than four in any public space or private house."

Alexander tightened his lips.

"And naiads will no longer be granted admittance to

the main section of the city except on business for a mer employer."

My body chilled. "Did he say what I think he just said?" I murmured.

"We've got to go to the quarter," said Alexander.

I nodded, but my whole body felt numb. I looked at Cassian. "Yes. It really looks like the king is going out of his way to protect the naiads."

"If I could just—"

"I'm busy," I snapped. "But if you give me a *very* compelling reason at a later time, I might hear you out." My gaze drifted to the sandy bottom of the canal. "Let's go," I said, tugging on Alexander's arm.

ALEXANDER AND I found Pippa in the growing crowd on Camford Canal.

"I thought you'd come," she said, opening her arms to hug me. "Everyone's in an uproar, as you can imagine."

"The murderers in the Guard should be held accountable," I said, "not the naiads."

Alexander pressed his hands together. "But that's not how the world works."

Pippa remained quiet.

"What will you do?" I rested my hand on her shoulder.

She hesitated. "That's what we're gathering together to find out."

"In defiance of the new law?"

"Well, we can't very well hide in our houses, can we?" she said. "Some of the Guard—soldiers known to be more loyal to Tor than to the king—burst into houses and dragged naiads into the canals to kill them."

"Barbaric," spat Alexander. "It really was a massacre, then."

"But we already knew that," I murmured. "We just didn't know the extent."

He scowled. "Well, now we know."

The crowd swelled, its discontented murmur growing with every passing moment.

Finally, Tryphaena—*Queen Tryphaena, by rights,* I reminded myself—hovered a few feet above the sandy coral to address the crowd, her waist-length white hair billowing around her.

"It seems we are at an impasse with the crown," she said, her voice cracking. "If we are no longer to be admitted to the part of the city in which the mer live, we cannot even bring our grievances to the king. It pains me to say that this break with Thessalonike must be made quickly and permanently, lest more devastation be wrought upon our people."

"So what must be done?" a dark-haired naiad called to Tryphaena.

"That is up to this crowd to decide. But I recommend that we leave Thessalonike behind and seek friendlier waters."

Someone grabbed me from behind.

"What's a mer doing in the naiad quarter today?" a male voice hissed in my ear.

Pippa turned and pushed a sandy-haired naiad off me. "Jade and Alexander are friends of our people."

Alexander looped his arms around my shoulders and glared at my assailant.

The sandy-haired naiad shoved Pippa backward. "No mer is a friend of the naiads. Not really. Besides," he said, looking at me more closely, "it's *her* fault all this happened."

I'd have preferred him to punch me in the stomach.

"So you think Tor should have gotten away with murdering my *sister*?" Pippa demanded.

He shrugged. "Maybe she was in on it. Maybe it's been a plot this whole time."

Pippa rolled her eyes. "If you believe that, you've been snorting too much puffer fish tincture."

I tried to ignore the belligerent naiad and focus on Tryphaena's conversation with the crowd. But I couldn't help watching out of the corner of my eye.

After another heated exchange with Pippa, the naiad stalked away. But I still couldn't relax. I'd had enough of being accosted in crowds, and in a sea of naiads, my tail and fin couldn't help but draw attention. I pulled Alexander's arms around me more tightly.

A young woman holding the hand of a small girl called out, "Where will we go?"

Tryphaena looked at her. "I don't know. I suggest we travel along the coast in the direction of Marbella. Perhaps we will find an accessible river system along the way. If no such system presents itself, Marbella may take us. If that fails, we must set out across the deep ocean in search of a new place to call home."

Murmurs ran through the crowd.

"Such a journey is dangerous. We must accept in advance that we will lose some of our people along the way."

The young woman picked up her daughter and clutched her to her chest.

"But," Tryphaena continued, "at the end of it, we may be lucky enough to find ourselves in a place where we can thrive. We've told ourselves for years that we're getting by, but in reality, this place is killing us one by one."

"What if we all die on the journey?" a male naiad called.

Tryphaena turned toward the speaker. "What if we all die here? The mer have been growing more and more antagonistic every year. If it's already come to a massacre in the canals, what hope do we have for our children?"

"We could fight back," he replied. "They're afraid of our water-casting for good reason. If we band together, they can't stop us."

Tryphaena shook her head. "I will not condone a course of action that leads inexorably to slaughter. We are powerful, but the mer outnumber us, and a civil war will devastate our people."

Pippa started playing with the edge of her watery, ethereal dress.

I leaned toward her, breaking out of Alexander's embrace. "What do you think?" I whispered, reaching back to squeeze Alexander's hand.

She bit her lip. "I know I thought about coming with you before, but I really don't think I can do it again."

"Can't do what again?"

"Flee my home in search of . . . what? The hope that there might be something better on the other side? What if it's not better? What if it's worse? Or we all die along the way?"

I placed a hand on her shoulder. "Is Thessalonike worse than the river system was?"

She pursed her lips and shook her head. "No. Not at the end. The river choked us out."

"Maybe this will be for the best, too."

She shot me a sharp look. "You want me to leave?"

I looked at Alexander. "We want to come with you."

She glanced from me to Alexander. "No, you don't."

"I'm serious. We can't stay. My reputation is too badly damaged, and we can't be together here. And really, we don't want to stay. Not after what the Guard did. Not after how the king let it go."

"But Jade, you've never had to leave your home behind. You don't want—"

I ran a hand through my hair. "You're right. I don't want to go. But the city is choking me out," I said.

Shaking her head, she said, "You have no idea what it's like. But—" Her gaze shifted from Alexander to me. "—I suppose that's not really my business."

"So it's settled," called Tryphaena over the crowd. "We

will move on and seek refuge somewhere beyond the walls of Thessalonike."

Excitement built in my chest. *This is it. Escape from the city.*

Pippa's shoulders slumped, and she looked down at the seafloor.

As the crowd dispersed, I reached out for her. "What is it?"

She shook off my hand. "I really appreciate everything you've tried to do. You're trying, and that's more than can be said for most of the mer in this city. But you really don't understand how much all of this hurts. You've never lost a sibling. You've never lost your home."

I drew back, startled. "I'm trying to understand."

"I—I'm not angry with you. Not exactly."

"Then what's wrong?"

"You need to know that you're voluntarily giving all of this up. You're not the one being pushed out."

"No one here wants *anything* to do with me." I hugged my arms over my chest. "I went to a party last night, and everyone snubbed me."

She rolled her eyes. "Tell me how much your feelings are hurt because posh people excluded you at a party."

I fell silent. "I'm sorry," I said at last. "That really sounded condescending of me, didn't it?"

"Yup." She offered me a wry smile. "You're pretty good at that." Then she reached her hand toward me. "I know you've lost a lot, too. I shouldn't minimize that."

"I shouldn't pretend it's on par with everything you've been through."

We met in a tight embrace, and when we pulled back, I shot a grin at Alexander. "Let's go with them."

"I'd like that," he said, squeezing my hand.

On our way back to my house, Alexander and I passed the canal Rhea lived on, and I hesitated.

"I . . . I think maybe I should stop in to see Rhea. And

offer her peace. I mean, I don't want to be her friend. But it doesn't matter if we're really leaving. Maybe it'll make the journey easier if I say goodbye."

He smiled at me, caressing my wrist with his fingers. "I think that's wise."

We turned toward Rhea's house, which lay along a row of small but well-maintained homes owned by nobles of lesser rank. I rapped on the door.

A dark-haired naiad servant answered, and his eyes widened. "How may I be of service, Lady Jade?"

I recognized him. He was the naiad I'd defended at the city gates the day Tor murdered Anna. "I'm here to see Rhea."

He bowed. "Of course, milady. I'll let her know."

He closed the door, and I turned to Alexander. "It's telling that I'm not granted admittance to the house."

He tucked my hair behind my ear. "You're doing the right thing."

The door opened again, and Rhea floated toward me.

"Hi Rhea," I said in a small voice.

"What are you doing here?" she asked, her voice quiet. She played with the ends of her hair, twisting the strands around and around her fingers.

"Good to see you, too," I said, wringing my hands together. "I came to wish you peace."

She swallowed. "Why?" Then she caught sight of Alexander over my shoulder. "Alexander. Um, hi. It's good to see you."

I grabbed his hand. "I know Yvonna threatened you."

Her gills flared, and she gripped the doorframe with white fingers. "You do?"

"Mother and Aunt Junia helped me put it all together. Listen, Alexander and I are engaged, and we'll be leaving the city soon."

Her hand flew to her mouth. "You're . . . what? How?"

I continued, "And I just wanted to let you know that I

don't bear you ill will for what happened at Tor's trial. I don't know that things could ever have been the same even if I didn't have to leave, but I didn't want you to think I hated you for the rest of our lives."

*Well, I do still hate her a little.* But she didn't need to know that.

"You're . . . engaged? To *Alexander?*"

*That's what she finds shocking?* "Yes. I am."

"Well," she said, blinking. "I . . . Does this mean Tor is fair game?"

I wanted to slap her, but Alexander squeezed my hand. "Tor has been *fair game* since the moment I broke up with him. But you should know he has a violent streak. Please don't entrust the rest of your life to him."

Her eyes narrowed. "I'll be the judge of that, but thanks for coming by. I appreciate it."

I paused. I'd humbled myself to reach out to her—to *apologize*—and she'd thrown it in my face. *Skub.*

"Well," I murmured. "That's all. I'm sorry I bothered you."

I turned around and started to swim away alongside Alexander.

"Jade!"

"What?" I asked without facing her.

"That was really immature of me. I'm sorry everything turned out this way."

I didn't say anything.

"You were a really loyal friend to me, and I shouldn't have betrayed that. It eats at me, you know. Every day."

"Thank you, Rhea," I said. I couldn't turn around lest she see my chin quivering.

"Go in peace." Her voice cracked.

"And peace be upon—" I couldn't finish the sentence. I looked over my shoulder and made eye contact with her.

She nodded and gave me a slight smile.

A KNOCK SOUNDED at my front door, and I turned toward Alexander with my eyebrows raised. There were few people in the city I wanted to talk to, and almost all of them had keys to the house.

He shrugged and mouthed, "Pippa?"

"Maybe. Or maybe Mother or Benjamin forgot the key." I moved to the door and swung it open.

Yvonna floated in the doorway, her face peaked and a silver cloak covering her hair.

I almost shut the door in her face. Instead, I crossed my arms. "Yes?"

She glanced up and down the canal. "Can I come in?"

I glared at her. "What gives you the right to—"

"Please." Her voice raised a full octave. "You were right. I have something for you."

I glanced at Alexander, who shrugged. "Let's hear her out."

*Because she's a conniving little shark.*

But I moved aside to allow her into the house. "You have exactly one minute to make this worth my time." I shut the door behind her.

Her voice returned to its normal pitch. "Now, I still think you're a disloyal little harpy and that you treated my son abominably."

I reached for the door handle.

"Wait." She held up her hands and moved toward the table. "I'm sorry. That wasn't diplomatic." She lowered herself into a hammock chair and folded her hands on the table.

"You can say that again." Alexander drummed his fingers together, his eyebrows arching.

Her gills flared. "What I mean to say is that I've disliked

your methods, and we clearly approach life from two different sets of values. But there are some things I cannot overlook."

I joined them at the table as Yvonna pulled a sheaf of tablets from underneath her cloak and passed them to me.

"I really did think you were lying about my husband's . . . involvement in the naiad disappearances."

Alexander glanced between Yvonna and me, but he kept quiet.

Yvonna straightened her back and stared at the blue coral wall. "But it made me think back to one or two things that didn't make sense over the last year." She steeled her gaze. "You and I may believe what we wish of each other, but I don't think either of us can sit idly by while girls are being sold."

# CHAPTER TWENTY-FOUR

I picked up the tablets. "What are you saying?"

"As I thought more about your accusation, I decided to look at a few of my husband's business records." She closed her eyes. "I found some things that shocked me. Horrified me. As a result, I've brought you some evidence you can take to the king. But I have one condition for you." Her eyes fluttered open, and determination flashed in her gaze.

I looked at Alexander, my mouth open. I didn't know what to say. Finally, I managed, "And your condition is?"

She stared at the tablets in my hand. "That you and Cleo handle this quietly with the king. I've brought you proof as a show of good faith. The fins of my husband's business endeavors must be trimmed, but I'd like to avoid another scandal. And I want him protected from public shame or expulsion. Swear to me that you'll try to keep this quiet, and the evidence is yours."

I narrowed my eyes. "Why don't you bring it to the king yourself?"

She held my gaze. "Which one of us has more leverage with the king right now?"

"You could come with me."

She shook her head. "I told you that I'm trying to keep this quiet. If you and I are seen together, rumors will swirl in the canals."

I floundered. "Or use your influence on Felix to get him to stop? I mean, you're his wife."

She hesitated and then lowered her cloak to her shoulders. She leaned forward, and the bioluminary light revealed a swollen gray bruise on her cheek. She whispered, "I've tried."

Quillpricks ran down my spine. *Like father, like son.*

Alexander shot upward. "Do you need help?"

She shook her head. "I'm fine."

"No, you're not," he said.

She tightened her jaw. "Leave it."

I threaded my fingers together. "How do I know this isn't another one of your schemes?" Something nagged at the back of my mind. What Benjamin had told me before the trial. "You . . . you're with the anti-monarchists. You met with Andronicus."

She shrugged. "I doubt I could prove my sincerity, but I've humiliated myself to give you a chance to stop the slaving, so I dearly hope my efforts don't go to waste. As far as the anti-monarchists go . . ." She paused and gazed at the wall. "Believe me or don't, but I'm on no one's side. That said, I believe it's good to have friends everywhere when the future's uncertain."

I hesitated. "The naiads are leaving the city. The trafficking will stop on its own."

Yvonna's eyes lit up.

"Most of them," said Alexander. "But not everyone. And if I were Felix, there's someone in particular I'd want gone."

I looked at him, and my whole body stilled. "Pippa."

He tilted his head. "She really sounded like she was thinking of staying. And she'll always be a threat to him. He can't act against her right away—too suspicious. But give it enough time . . ."

I clutched the tablets to my chest with my left hand and reached out my right and grasped Yvonna's forearm. "I swear that I'll try my best to keep this quiet. Though if it comes down to saving a naiad or shielding your husband, I'll save the naiad every time. The trafficking will end, and we'll get back the girls who have already been sold."

We squeezed each other's forearms to seal the oath.

"Very well." She released my arm and rose from the hammock chair, pulling her cloak back around her face.

I floated toward the door alongside her. "Tides keep you safe. Are you sure you don't need help?"

She opened the door. "Despite everything he's done, I love my husband. Worry about your naiad friends; I'll worry about my marriage." With another glance up and down the canal, she swam away.

---

"I'LL TREAT YOU like a child if you insist on acting like one," Mother said, her hands on her hips.

"I'm of age. And I've grown up a lot these last few weeks. You said so yourself. Besides, if I was old enough to make a decision about marrying and then breaking things off with Tor, I'm old enough to make a decision about starting a new life with Alexander. I know Alexander a lot better than I ever knew Tor." *And I haven't even broached the conversation about Yvonna and the tablets yet.* I groaned.

Alexander floated at my side, not saying anything. He knew my mother well enough to know it wouldn't do either of us any good.

"With all due respect to Alexander," Mother said, "and whether or not he's a good match for you, you cannot leave Thessalonike right now."

"Why not?" I folded my arms across my chest and looked her in the eye.

"For the greater good."

"That's what the king said when he tried to pressure me to marry Tor."

Mother glanced at the coral floor. "I've sheltered you from a lot of the politics in this city. I always wanted you to feel secure. But, as you said, you've grown up a lot recently."

A tendril of dread curled in my stomach. "What?"

"It's a dangerous time for the nobility, especially for those of us who are closely aligned with the king. The king is growing paranoid. Protests in the canals have swelled."

I wondered if she was talking about Andronicus.

"Alexander, could you give us a few minutes?" she asked.

I clutched his hand tighter. "Anything you want to say to me, you can say in front of Alexander. We're getting married."

Mother rolled her eyes and shot a biting look at Alexander.

He untangled his fingers from mine and gave me an apologetic look. "I'll be back soon."

I sighed and crossed my arms over my chest as he slipped out of the house and into the canal.

"What?" I demanded, facing Mother.

"The king is anticipating a major coup attempt, perhaps in the next year. He's making preparations to ensure the Guard halt it decisively."

I felt sure all the color had drained from my face. "What are you talking about? That—that can't be. We haven't had a coup for centuries. Not since the days of Queen Jade."

"King Stephanos is not as strong a leader as his mother or grandfather were," she said. "And when poor Elias eventually takes the throne, I can only imagine how quickly the dynasty will dissolve."

I blinked. "Elias isn't clever, to be sure, but are things really as bad as all that?"

"I'm afraid so." She crossed to the open window and stared out at the bustling canal. "As you know, our family is inextricably intertwined with the monarchy. If things stay as they are, when it falls, we'll be dragged down to the depths with it. Perhaps literally."

I sank into one of the hammocks at the dining room table. "Why are you telling me all this?"

Her gills pulsed. "I don't think the king's motives were all bad when he asked you to marry Tor."

"There's no—"

She held up her hand. "Calm yourself. I'm not saying he had the right to ask it of you. In part, I do believe he wanted to protect you as best he could by marrying you off to a powerful family in the city that is not wholly aligned with him.

"Tor's family is unlikely to be hurt in a revolution. In fact, they stand a good chance of emerging from the violence more powerful than before. But, at the same time, many of the king's motivations were selfish. Now that Elias has eloped with a fisher's daughter, the king only has a single child with which to make a suitable match with a good family. So, I think he decided to use you as a surrogate princess. If you are a member of Felix's family, Felix is less likely to support a revolt. And Felix is one of the most influential nobles in the hierarchy."

Realization dawned on me. "Cassian works for the king."

"Who?" Mother asked.

"Cassian. That merman who attacked Aunt Junia and me in city center."

Mother rubbed the back of her neck. "I'm afraid he does. Another detail the king didn't see fit to inform me of until afterward."

"He's trying to blackmail Felix," I said. "He's not actually interested in stopping Felix from kidnapping naiads. He just wants to be able to threaten Felix into compliance." I felt a rush of relief that I hadn't handed over the tablet.

"What are you talking about?" Mother asked.

"Felix is selling naiads to overlanders. I-I have evidence."

Her eyebrows knitted together. "Well, the king told me

that Cassian had accosted you by mistake. I see that he and I may have much to discuss." Her voice had grown icy.

*I would not want to be the king in that conversation.* I almost laughed.

She shook her head. "If you leave with the naiads and your new fiancé, after everything that's happened . . . I know that you and Alexander didn't rekindle your romance until after the murder, but will the public believe that?"

I thought of the way Kora's face had flushed when she'd rushed to tell me of Lady Penelope's affair with the ambassador.

"No," I whispered. "They live for scandal."

"Where do you think that will leave your brother?"

I tightened my lips.

"Your Aunt Junia and I are both getting older. But Benjamin? The best hope for both of you is that you'll each marry into a family whose tide is rising, not ebbing. And do you think there's any chance of that for Benjamin if you disappear with Alexander so soon after Tor's trial?"

I didn't know what to say.

The stern lines around her eyes softened. "I'm sorry. It's unfair that you have to make this kind of decision. Perhaps I'm as bad as the king."

*But it's true.* I knew it deep in my being.

"No," I murmured. "You're just trying to protect Benjamin as best as you can."

"And if you stay . . ." She trailed off.

"I can't marry Alexander."

"Well, maybe someday," she said. "In three or four years, perhaps. It would be better if you waited until Benjamin's had a chance to make a good match, though. If you're insistent on marrying Alexander, the pressure of finding powerful allies falls to Benjamin, and how many families will want their daughters tied to us if you've married a laborer?"

Rubbing the back of my neck, I murmured, "Our value

is measured by our proximity to the king. If the monarchy begins to crack . . ."

She nodded. "As the king grows weaker, our family's name becomes less valuable. If the king is ousted, or if he dies and Elias takes the throne and cannot manage the city, what benefit will a match with us give to another family?"

"But if I'm still single and flirting at parties, and it seems like an engagement with Philip or Damian may be forthcoming, it's easier for Benjamin to make a match."

"It's an unfair situation," said Mother, "but you see how much pressure it puts on Benjamin if you've eliminated the hope of a good connection for yourself."

My throat tightened. "That would be a lot for anyone."

"Yes. It would be."

I buried my face in my hands.

Mother floated behind me and rubbed my shoulders. "Did you never wonder why I discouraged Alexander when the two of you were in school? You know the politicking and ostentation displayed by so many of the nobles disgusts me. I've never personally disliked the boy."

"I get it," I said. "You've always known it might come to this."

We fell silent for a few minutes.

I pulled my head back up. "What if we all go with the naiads? Start over in Marbella, or somewhere new?"

Mother's face remained impassive. "Aunt Junia couldn't make the journey. It's dangerous, and with her fatigue . . . the physicians say it's enervia. It won't kill her, but she's not going to get better, either."

I looked down at the floor.

"She wouldn't be able to swim that far, let alone fight the currents," Mother said.

My heart plummeted to my stomach. "Perhaps I could fake my death and sneak away at night."

Mother raised her eyebrows. "Listen to yourself."

I stared at my hands.

"You're right, Jade. You're of age. It's your choice. But you need to take stock of the lives you're impacting before you make decisions you can't reverse."

The door opened, and Benjamin floated in, clutching his bag tightly to his chest. His eyes were wide. "Have you heard?" he asked, darting toward me.

"About the naiad restrictions?"

He nodded.

I sighed. "I'm afraid I have."

"It's not fair!" He dropped his bag. "Why do mer hate the naiads so much?"

I didn't have the energy to explain the messy, complicated history, so I just said, "There are a lot of reasons. But I think it all started because mer were afraid of the naiads' magic. Water-casting is powerful."

He crossed his arms over his chest. "Well, that's stupid. If we're afraid of the naiads taking over our city, shouldn't we treat them well so they're our friends?"

*If only the world were so simple.* But I didn't have the heart to say that to him. Instead, I said, "It looks like the naiads are going to leave the city even though they haven't been banished."

He stiffened. "You can't be serious."

"I heard it from Tryphaena herself."

He shook his head.

"It's better this way," I said. "How were they supposed to stay with so many mer against them? More naiads would've gotten hurt."

He pulled away from me. "Still—"

"I know. I know. I hate it, too." *More than you know.*

"When will they leave?"

"I don't know." I ran both my hands through my hair. "Soon, I think. I'm sure it will take them a few days to gather themselves."

"Where will they go?" he asked. "Back to the rivers?"

"Maybe," I said. "Or Marbella, if they can get there."

He nodded. "Julius's father is a merchant who travels between Thessalonike and Marbella. He says there are some naiads there. Cecaelias and kelpies, too. But I don't know about that. I'm not sure kelpies really exist." He clasped his hands together. "I hope they'll be alright."

"We'll all be alright," I said.

His face froze. "You're going with them, aren't you? You and Alexander?"

I closed my eyes. "No. Now go get changed. School wraps are depths uncomfortable."

"Are you okay?"

"I just need a moment with Mother."

"You know I can hear everything from my room."

"Don't eavesdrop this time." I put my hand on his arm. "Please."

He took in my serious expression and nodded. "Just this once. I'll be down in a minute." He darted up the corridor.

I turned and met Mother's intense gaze. "I'll stay," I whispered, pushing myself up from the table. "For his sake. Let me go find Alexander and tell him."

She grasped my shoulder. "That's a very selfless and brave choice."

"He's my baby brother." I squeezed her hand. "And we've got to stick together."

I slipped out of the house before Benjamin came back down.

"Hey." Alexander swam toward me. He'd been loitering three doorways away. "Are you okay?"

My chin quivered. "No."

His jaw tightened. "What happened? What did she say to you?"

My voice wavered as I told him about the conversation, but I managed to keep my sobs at bay.

"I see," he said when I finished. "So what you're saying is, you want me to stay here—but I can't be with you—in hopes that we can marry in several years?"

I looked down. "I'll understand if you can't stay."

He ran a hand through his hair. "Can you guarantee me that we can get married if I stay here and wait for you?"

I swallowed. "I—I hope so. I want to. But . . ."

"But what?"

"Depths, Alexander." My gills pulsed. "I love you."

He pulled me into his chest. "I love you, too. Always."

"It's just . . ." I put a hand over my mouth to still a sob as I backed out of his embrace. "If things go as badly as Mother expects them to . . . I won't let Benjamin or Aunt Junia get hurt by refusing to marry someone who can shield them. I can't. I can't do that."

He scoffed. "So you'll protect the king at whatever cost."

I wrapped my arms around myself to try to quiet the webbed-foot dragon raging in my chest. "The king has nothing to do with this." I hiccupped. "He can sink under the weight of his own beard for all I care."

Alexander said nothing.

"But my family. I've made them *very* unpopular as of late. If I have to fix that by committing myself to someone I don't love, I will."

He grabbed my hand. "If your father were alive—"

An eerie calm washed over me, like a double-strength puffer fish tincture had washed over my gills. "It wouldn't make a difference. Mother's social status was higher than his when they married. It's her influence that catapulted us to prominence."

"It might not make a difference to your circumstances, but he wouldn't let you do this to yourself."

I shook my head. "You're wrong. My father died trying to protect naiads he didn't even know."

He pulled me close to his chest and caressed my hair.

"I have nothing but you to stay for, Jade. But I will." He dropped a kiss on the top of my head.

My stomach roiled, and I panicked again. "But what if you wait for me just to watch me marry someone else?"

"Maybe you won't have to. I mean, Yvonna literally handed you blackmail on Felix. Surely we could use that somehow, to . . ."

"To what?" I threw out my hands. "It's not just Felix we're fighting. It's the anti-monarchists and a big chunk of the nobles, and who knows how many mer my mother's angered over the years."

Cold certainty plunged through my chest like a sinking ship. *I can't do this to him.*

"No," I whispered. "I love you too much to put you through four years of waiting and then force you to watch me marry someone else."

He let me go and floated backward to look me in the eye. "You're sure that's where it ends?" he asked, his voice strangled.

"Yeah," I whispered, forcing back a sob. "Sure enough."

His gills flared, and he closed his eyes. "Well, then."

"I'm so sorry," I murmured.

He reached out to pull me close and kissed me on the forehead. "I'm sorry, too. But if I'm just going to lose you again, we may as well make a clean break." He held me. "And I'll need to get away from the memories."

"Wait." I reached up to caress his face, my fingers tingling. "You don't have to leave with the naiads. I'm not saying you have to wait five years for me. And if you meet another girl, that's okay, but surely—" My voice cracked. "—we can give it a few months? A year? See what happens with the anti-monarchists?"

He shook his head. "I can't. Depths, Jade, don't you see? You're so fixated on doing the right thing that we'll never be together."

"How do—"

"Your martyr complex won't allow it."

I drew back, and my voice sharpened. "My . . . martyr complex?"

"You overthink every little thing because for some reason you don't think you deserve to be happy. Well, guess what? You're not the only one in this relationship. And if you won't let yourself be happy, that affects me, too."

We stared at each other, and my face crumpled.

"I'm sorry," he said. "If I really thought there was a chance, I'd stay."

"I know," I whispered. "Go in peace."

He bowed. "And peace be upon you."

I thought my heart would shatter when he swam away, his fin flapping in slow, halfhearted jerks. *Goodbye.*

After he disappeared around the corner, I made my way back to the house. When I opened the door, Mother pulled me into her arms, and I sobbed into her shoulder until I didn't feel anything anymore.

AS THE FIRST rays of sun cut through the waves two mornings later, I heard a soft knock on the door. I didn't stir from my place at the table. Mother answered the door.

"Pippa?" she said. "Do come in."

I looked up. "Hey," I said softly.

She set her basket down and shifted from foot to foot. "I—I told the guards that I was bringing mending back to you. Just in case they ask you about it later."

Mother nodded. "Of course we'll vouch for you. Are you okay?"

"Yes. Yes, of course. I've come to ask a favor."

"Anything you need," I said, my voice cracking. I stopped

and cleared my throat. "Anything at all." My voice was stronger this time.

She played with the hem of her dress. "I can't move on with everyone. I can't set out and hope that we find something better. I was wondering if I might be able to stay in Thessalonike, under your employment. I know it's a lot to ask, but I don't know that other mer will give me any work after—"

"Done," said Mother. "And you'll live with us so that you won't be accosted moving back and forth between the naiad quarter—or, I suppose, what will have once been the naiad quarter—and our home."

Her eyes widened. "Are you sure? I don't want to impose."

"We have three extra sleeping chambers." Mother waved her hand. "And while I can't promise that we'll be able to keep you safe forever, I think the people's anger at the naiads will ebb once the main group leaves. I'm sure I can persuade the king to drop these ridiculous restrictions by the time the year is out, especially if there aren't many naiads remaining in the city."

"I think only about two dozen of us mean to stay," she said. "Even the elderly are going. They'll lose a lot of them on the journey, I'm afraid."

Mother's shoulders drooped for a moment. "I'm sorry to hear that."

"Do you know if Alexander is going with them?" I asked.

She hesitated for a moment. "Yes. About five mer are going. Mer who lived in the naiad quarter for a long time and have built their lives with us. Alexander is among them."

Even though I'd expected it, the news plunged into my chest like a blade. I rested my cheeks in my hands and stared at the floor.

Mother reached her hand out toward me. "It's for the best. It's better that he moves on. That way, you can, too."

Pippa held out a tablet wrapped in seaweed. "He wanted me to give you this message."

I grabbed it from her and held it tightly in my hands, but

I couldn't bear to look at it. I tucked it under my arm to read later, in private. "Thank you for bringing it to me. Could you excuse me a minute?"

"Of course," she said.

Mother glanced at the tide glass. "Don't take too long. We have our audience with the king in an hour to discuss the tablets Yvonna brought you."

Pippa raised an eyebrow, and Mother waved me up the corridor as she began recounting the pieces of the story Pippa hadn't yet heard.

I fled up the corridor. When I reached my room, I hesitated for a moment at the window, staring toward the walls of the city and wondering if he'd stay if I rushed to the quarter and begged him to change his mind.

But I couldn't.

I unwrapped the tablet.

*My dearest Jade,*

*I couldn't leave without saying goodbye, but I didn't trust myself to be able to do it in person without begging you to come with me. As I told you once, my whole heart has always been, and ever will be, yours, but I want you to know that I understand.*

*You defend those you care about. It's in your nature. And I know you wouldn't be able to live with yourself if you were always worried about the people you love back in Thessalonike, wondering if you'd endangered them.*

*I have to go—not just for myself, but so that you don't have to live torn between love and duty. Please understand that I leave with no ill will and only the sort of passing anger that vanishes in a strong current.*

*May the tides keep you safe, and I wish you only joy.*

*With all my heart, Alexander.*

I pressed the tablet to my lips and stared out the window again. "I love you," I whispered. "Go in peace."

After a few minutes, I glanced at the tide glass and tucked the tablet in the drawer next to my dolphin pendant. With my head held high, I floated back down.

"Thank you," I said to Pippa, my voice still unsteady.

She smiled softly at me.

Another knock sounded on the door. This time, I answered it.

Maximus floated there in full guard regalia, his fingers clutching the handle of his club.

I pulled myself up short. "Oh. Hi. What are you doing here?"

He opened and closed his mouth.

I went cold. "What is it?"

"The king wishes to summon Lady Cleo immediately," he said. "Yvonna's been killed."

# ACKNOWLEDGMENTS

It's daunting to sit down and set out to thank everyone who's made this book possible because so many people have supported and inspired me along the way.

Brendan—Your support has meant the world. You were so understanding when I said I had to quit my day job to focus on writing and editing, and you've never looked back.

Mom—You live for your children and grandchildren, and you encouraged and funded so many opportunities. You once purchased forty hardcovers to qualify me to go to a writers' conference, and it was at that conference that I started making the critical connections that gave me a career in this industry. And who knew how useful swimming with dolphins would end up being?

Brittany—Thanks so much for being my favorite sister. I trust your judgment implicitly, and your support over the years has been such an encouragement. Also, thanks for your last-minute catches in *Breakwater*!

Stephanie, Jessica, and Brielle—I love you ladies so much. You make my life better in every way.

My kitties, Mildred and Minerva—You worked tirelessly to introduce typos at every possible moment. I admire your dedication to walking on my keyboard.

My editors, Ben Wolf, Christabel Barry, Stephanie Guido, Jacqueline Frasca, Veronica Meredith, and Chelsea Tatum—I've relied on each and every one of you to make this novel work. Bit by bit you've taken this book from a messy, underdeveloped, inconsistent draft into the novel it is today. You're the dream team.

Kirk DouPonce—The cover is perfect. I feel so lucky to have worked with such a talented artist, and I can't wait to see what you do with the rest of the series.

Chris Bell—For all the advice and, of course, your top-notch interior design skills, I am so grateful.

Davis Bunn—If you hadn't taken the time to sit down and troubleshoot my biggest writing hurdle, I don't know that I would have ever finished the first draft.

Rachel—You were the very first writer to entrust me with editing a real book manuscript, and that launched the journey that made it feel possible for me to publish *Breakwater*. Your stories inspire me, and your prose is captivating. I'm so thrilled we're both releasing our debuts this year.

Katie—Oh, what can I say in this amount of space? Your infectious positivity and desire to see those around you succeed makes the lives of everyone you touch better. You pretty much singlehandedly kept me in the indie publishing industry when it seemed easier to just work a day job, and I have adored each and every one of your stories.

My online writing communities, especially AfE, the blue monkeys, RWM, and Realm Makers Consortium—At varying times in this journey, you've kept me sane, motivated me, and pointed me in the right direction.

My co-conspirators—Andrew, Avily, Ben, Charis, Becky, Scott, Lindsay, Nadine, Sarah, and Teddi. You keep me on track, talk me down when I get in my own head, and always encourage me toward excellence. Let's take over the world.

Made in the USA
Columbia, SC
13 June 2017